Dedication

To Rick, for Being Patient

To Ashley Reynolds, My Memory and My PIC

To Alex M. Turner, My Mark Moretti and My Muse

Prologue
10 years ago

"Moretti, let's wrap it up man." Rich Dickerman pounded his fist on the side of the Chevy Equinox with the steam covered windows. "Five minutes until first pitch. Let's get a move on." Rich paced the length of the car. His role as look out was getting old. He couldn't wait for the day Mark Moretti decided life was not just one party after another. He would be there on the sidelines laughing. "Ha," he chuckled.

The car door opened and Mark stepped out. Tucking his jersey back into his pants, he turned and flashed his million dollar smile at the sophomore brunette in the back seat. "Thanks, Kelly." He slammed the door shut.

"It's Casey." Rich shoved Mark and laughed. "Not Kelly. Casey."

"Kelly, Casey, same thing." Mark stretched his pitching arm.

"It is not even close to the same thing. You really are a pig. I'm not sure I understand how you do it. Are these women dumb?" Rich threw him the baseball.

Mark stopped for a minute. He shook his head and smiled. "Dumb? Hardly. I am a good investment. Besides, every one of them thinks they can change me. That's never going to happen. But I thoroughly enjoy their attempts."

Mark threw the baseball to Rich. This was the last game of their senior season. Hard to believe they would be graduating in a week. He had heard that the high school years were some of the best. They had been good to him. But soon, he would pack up his life and move into a tiny apartment outside the UCLA campus with Caleb and Ryan. Rich would go to his fancy, private school and Molly would be left behind to carry on the Moretti name.

He sighed. Molly. Sweet, beautiful, innocent Molly. Life had not been easy for them. The military demanded constant moving and Mario Moretti had not wanted his children torn away from what they knew. So he headed out on adventures all over the world, leaving his wife and two children behind to struggle to keep up with the socialites of Beverly Hills. Mark had worked as long as he could remember. He wanted Molly to be able to join clubs and have friends and not worry about how she would pay for things. At the age of ten, Mark had vowed to make enough money to care for everyone he loved. That list was short but significant.

Rich Dickerman, Caleb Allen and Mark Moretti were the bad boys of Beverly Hills. Or so they thought. Where one was seen, the other two were sure to follow. They were the three musketeers until Ryan West crash landed smack into the mix in middle school. Rich was level headed and the voice of reason while Caleb broke some hearts and even more rules. Ryan and Mark were the best of both. Both studious and rebellious, they spent their weekends chasing women, stealing beer from their parent's refrigerator and studying. The four of them had been joined at the hip until Rich fell in love with Molly Moretti. Mark loved his sister more than anything in the world. He welcomed her into the fold with open arms. But there was nothing like a younger sister to ruin someone's game.

Mark made his way to the pitching mound. The sun had set and the lights hummed above him as he took some calming breaths. His last varsity baseball game. He threw several pitches to the catcher to loosen his arm. He inventoried his friends, as he did the beginning of every game. Rich on first, Ryan at center field and Caleb in his soccer gear sitting in the stands next to Molls, his beautiful sister. All was right in the world.

"Play Ball"

Mark sat in the dugout at the end of the game. Molly sat on Rich's lap and Mark shook his head. "That's my sister, man. Cool it."

"Marco, I take it those are yours?" Caleb laughed as he pointed to the row of women sitting in the stands.

Mark looked up as a few of them waved. He winked and waved back. It was good to be him. "None of them are mine C. But they all want to be."

He chuckled as he packed up his gear.

"Give me a break." Molly smacked him on the leg. "There will come a day that some woman steals your heart, Markie. And I cannot wait until that happens. Pay back is a huge bitch."

"I agree, Moretti. When that day comes, I am strapping myself in because it's going to be one hell of a ride."

Mark laughed and looked his friends in the eye. "That day will never come. I am Mark Moretti. Forever a bachelor."

Chapter One

"Always the one with the broken wheel. Always!" Sophie huffed as she blew at a strand of her blond hair that had escaped from her messy bun. She knew Saturday morning was the worst time to shop. But with her work week ending later that expected and the engagement party only a few hours away, she knew she only had time for a quick work out and an even quicker trip to the grocery store.

She loathed grocery shopping. Actually, she loathed shopping of any kind. It wasn't until she met Molly six months ago that her views on shopping had changed. And they had changed by force.

Six months ago, Sophie had made the move to Los Angeles to follow her college boyfriend. She had landed her dream job editing for Phantom House books and loved being a junior editor. They had bought a tiny house with a yard full of stones and she had hung some flower baskets and made herself a little sanctuary in back. A month into her job, she had come home early with a headache and walked into her worst nightmare. Shawn had brought his secretary home and was enjoying her in the bed they shared. After several screaming matches, she had learned of Shawn's indiscretions during their four year relationship. She packed a few suitcases and walked away from the future she had written for herself.

Molly had been a mentor at work and had been her only true girlfriend in the whole city. The few friends she had made with Shawn found him more entertaining and had turned their backs on her the moment they heard the news. Molly had saved her. Sophie moved into the tiny apartment Molly was leaving to move in with her fiancé. She had forced Sophie from her funk by signing them up for Pilates and taking her to the spa for a complete life overhaul. She forced Sophie to throw away the remainders of her old life by taking her shopping for furniture and clothing and refused to let her sulk on Friday nights. On one occasion, she had even taken her speed dating to try to open her eyes to other men in the world. She was her rock and Sophie knew she would not have made it through the last six months without her.

The buzzing of her phone brought her back to reality as she fished through her giant purse to find it. The envelope alerted her to the text message.

"Babes! I need you to get over here stat! My cousin just found out she is pregnant and I need a new Maid of Honor. Dress fitting in one hour. See you there."

Sophie just stared at the phone. She was happy for Molly, but part of her died a little every time she was reminded of how happy her best friend was. Her self confidence had stayed back in the old house when she walked away from it. She questioned her decisions, her looks, and her desire to ever find a man again.

Her cart hit something hard and it stopped with a jolt. Sophie looked up and saw she had run into a man's heels. "I am so sorry. Oh my gosh. Are you ok?"

He turned around with a small huff and looked down at her. He pulled his baseball cap off his head and ran his hand through his dark hair. "Well, you are going to owe me some Band-Aids." His grin reached his green eyes and Sophie couldn't help but smile. "And if I didn't have somewhere to be five minutes ago, I would wait." He laughed as he started to jog away.

"It was nice running into you." Before she had a chance to

think, the words were out of her mouth. She had never seen anyone so handsome before. Of course, she had shown her true clumsy colors and rammed him with the cart. Sighing, she looked at her watch and picked up her pace. She needed to get out of here and across town to put on a dress that would remind her again what a failure her relationship had been.

****

Mark settled into his new car and shook his head. What was that? He had taken one look at this frazzled woman and his heart had jumped into his throat. *Enough Moretti, get it together* he told himself as he put the key in the ignition.

Rich was going to kill him. He was supposed to be at the tux shop by now and he had yet to pick up the kegs for the party tonight. His first night back in LA had been a little wild and running into his high school sweetheart had been an added bonus. The shocking part was waking up in her bed this morning. He knew things might be a little awkward tonight since she was part of the bridal party and he needed to set things straight as soon as he saw her.

His decision to join the Marines right after graduating from UCLA had taught him a few valuable lessons. He was always a gentleman but he was not the marrying kind. He had seen his buddies lose their girlfriends and wives while they were away for so long on tour and he refused to put himself in that situation. He had tried when his tour was over but each time he met someone, his heart wasn't in it. He was happy being a bachelor and he knew his decision to move back to LA would only confirm that for him. He was living the high life being a stock broker and his transfer to the corporate headquarters gave him the corner office with the view he'd been working so hard for. He would not have time to share life with anyone.

He cursed as he reached Rich's voicemail for the third time. "I swear I am not blowing you off Man. I got caught up this morning. It's a long story that you won't be hearing because Molly will kill me. But I will see you soon." He tossed his phone onto the passenger seat.

He had time for one stop.
Missing either would make
Rich panic but only one would
ruin the whole night. He needed
to get the kegs.

****

Sophie looked around the
grounds in awe. The vast
backyard was perfectly
groomed and caterers raced
around making sure everything
was perfect. The pool was lit
with floating candles and there
were flowers everywhere. She
looked down at her black
sundress and sandals and
suddenly felt very
underdressed. She knew Rich
came from money but she had
no idea what that meant until
now. She felt guilty for not
paying more attention to
Molly's description of what

Rich's life had been like. She shivered wondering what the wedding would be like if this was only an engagement party.

"A friendly face!" Molly squealed behind her.

Sophie crossed her arms across her chest. "Next time you invite me over, could you give me a specific dress code? What is all this?"

Molly giggled, "This babes, is my new life. Look around. This is the uncomfortable place I will be bringing my children for holidays. I don't even know half these people." She took a long swig of her champagne. "Rumor has it my brother has snuck a few kegs in the side yard so if this isn't your scene…"

"Lead the way." Sophie followed Molly through the maze of people in designer clothing and big hats.

Molly had hit the jackpot with Rich. He was a wonderful man; He held doors open for her and spent Sundays in pajama pants reading the paper and doing the crossword with her in his lap. He was classically handsome, tall, blond and very boy next door. The modest home they had purchased proved to Sophie that he was not being influenced by his parent's money. Until today, she would have never guessed Rich was LA royalty.

The sounds of the party became a little more rowdy as they rounded the estate. She sighed in relief thinking she would fit in a little better here.

"Marco!" Rich yelled from the center of the crowd.
"Dickerman!" The two men embraced before Rich playfully smacked the side of his head. "Where were you man? I hope this thing fits you because I am not going back there."

The dark haired man looked smug. "Look, tux or kegs. Which is more important right now?"

"Ask my mom the same question on the wedding day when your pants are two sizes too small."

"I think your mom will think I made the right choice if that's the case." He laughed, earning another smack on the head.

"Markie!!" Molly took off running into the arms of the dark haired stranger. He kissed her and spun her in a circle a few times before kissing her again. She buried her face into his chest and started crying.

"Shh Molls. I'm back and I'm not going anywhere." He whispered as he kissed the top of her head and stepped back to look her in the eyes. "I need you to answer a serious question baby. Are you sure you want to marry this putz?" Another smack. "I really think you could do better. I mean, seriously, look at this dump. They haven't kept it up at all over the years."

Molly laughed and snuggled in again. Sophie stood back about 6 feet just watching her with this handsome man. His linen pants hung just perfectly on his hips and his un-tucked white shirt showed off his tanned and extremely toned arms. Her stomach fluttered as she stared at him. What was wrong with her? *Reality check*, she told herself. *This guy is so far out of your league.* She tried to will her hands to stop sweating when his piercing green eyes met hers.

"Band-aide girl?" He asked.

Sophie blushed. She hadn't recognized him. Her voice cracked and surprised her. "That would be me."

"You know each other?" Molly looked confused.

"No. Not officially," He stepped forward and extended

his hand. "I'm Mark, Best Man. Which goes without saying." Something happened when he touched her. He looked down at their hands.

The giggle had been unexpected. Sophie cleared her throat, "I'm Sophie, Maid of Honor as of this morning." A jolt of energy shot up her arm just from a simple handshake. She shook her head to clear her mind.

"The notorious Sophie. Nice to meet you. Molls is always too busy to talk to me because she's busy with Sophie." Mark smiled. Sophie blushed and looked at the ground. Yep. Just another reminder of how needy she had become.

Taking full advantage of the loss of eye contact, Mark let his eyes roam freely over the Maid of Honor. She had affected him this morning and now his whole body tightened at seeing her. She was pretty. Her long blond hair was down and curled loosely over her shoulders. Her eyes were dark brown and set off by thick lashes. He looked at her mouth and wondered what it would be like to kiss such full lips. Her baggy clothes hid her body and she was shy, made obvious by the blush. *She's out of the question*, he told himself. This was Molly's best friend and that was a line he couldn't cross without hurting his sister.

Noticing her friend's face, Molly stepped forward. "Ignore him. He hardly calls. And I can't help it that I enjoy her company more than yours."

Mark acted like he'd been stabbed. "Fine baby but just remember I was your first love."

Speaking of first loves, Mark noticed Amber making her way to him. "Oh shit," he muttered. "Who wants a beer?" He quickly turned around and made a bee line toward the keg.

"Oh shit what? What did you do Mark?" Molly saw Amber's face light up when she saw him. This was not going to be good. "Mark?"

Sophie looked toward the cute red head she had met at the bridal salon today. The girl had been a little nervous this morning but she looked confident and happy tonight. "What's up with Mr. Ripped and Amber?"

"Eww. Please don't call him that." She made a face. "Amber was Mark's first, well, whatever she was. They dated for three years in high school. He wasn't the best boyfriend. Then again…" Her voice trailed off as Amber passed her and walked toward Mark. "Amber is engaged to Steve, one of this crazy Dickerman gang from high school. They were the boys all the girls wanted to date. Sadly, my friends all wanted too also. She told me she ran into Mark last night at a club. I didn't think anything of it. But Mark's reaction just told me everything. This is gonna get ugly."

Amber walked right past Mark and gave Steve the most intimate kiss Sophie had ever

seen. Mark's jaw dropped.
"Yes it is."

****

Sophie looked over the 'Dickerman gang' and could see why they had been the bad boys of high school. Rich was the classic boy next door, probably had the good grades and grew up in an amazing home. Steve was clean cut but you could tell by his eyes that he had a devious side. Chad was now a teacher at the same school where he had spent his years torturing the poor and unfortunate educators that had the pleasure of teaching this rowdy bunch. Ryan was your classic bad boy, covered in tattoos, personal trainer to the stars, muscles that went on for miles and the looks women couldn't leave alone. Then there was Caleb, her sweet friend Caleb. Sophie smiled at him. She had been told once that he had been the wild one of the group but his calm and loving personality told her that either no one really knew him, or he had changed significantly since their high school days. Then there was Mark. Sophie blushed. Mr. Sex on a stick. He was a hunk. His 6'3" frame and jet black messy hair was set off by his piercing green eyes and olive complexion. He had bad boy written all over him. Heat pooled between her legs just looking at him.

Her thoughts were interrupted when Rich stepped onto the picnic table and raised his glass to get the bridal party's attention. "I really want to thank all you guys for being a part of our wedding day. You know my mother so you know this whole wedding is going to be totally out of control. That being said, Molly and I just want you all to know how much it means to us that you decided to accept our offer to be a part of this craziness." Rich stepped down and opened a large box lying under the picnic table as molly pulled another one out from the other side. "Most of us have been friends for our whole lives, and our new additions just make our group that much better. We didn't think a flask or whatever it is you girls give each other was enough to tell you all how special you are to us. I have been more than blessed with what life has given me and I have gotten to spend the last ten years convincing Molly none of this matters to me. I can't wait to make her my wife."

The girls in the crowd melted as the guys moaned and yelled "whipped" and laughed.

Molly shook her head. "Ok Ok. Calm Down. We have less than a month until the wedding and I know you guys are in for some hell between then and now. What Rich is trying to say is that we love you guys and we didn't mind using a little of his family's…umm blessings? to help us show you that. We know this wedding is going to be nuts and we want to be able to spend some time with you guys with no stress and no schedule…" her voice trailed off as she yanked a carry on bag out of the box. "So we got you all a gift we think you can use. And when you open this, don't panic because Rich's very helpful mother has already been in contact with wives, husbands, bosses, and whoever else she needed to get clearance from…"

Sophie took a bag from Rich's hand and slowly opened the zipper. Peering into her bag, the first thing that caught her eye was the pair of flip flops and the beach towel. Pulling the towel from the bag, she noticed the tiny pink bikini and the sealed envelope. People began cheering and high fiving. She tore open the envelope to see what it was. Staring back at her was a round trip plane ticket for Negril, Jamaica. Printed on it was the name Sophie Barringer and May 6 – May 10, two days from now. Sophie's breath caught as she saw the brochure for the hotel.

"Hedonism? Holy Hell Dickerman. Seriously?" Stunned, Mark looked up at his sister and Rich.

"Guess we will finally find out if the infamous Marco is a Prude or a Nude." Rich laughed as he kissed Molly gently and smiled.

Chapter 2

"What's up Marco?" Chad threw his carry on above his head and took the window seat right next to Mark. "First class dude. This is a first for me."

"Man, I need this. I haven't taken any time since the week I took between my last tour and my first day on the job. Unfortunately, I have got to get some work done on the plane". Mark started laughing, "Little Molly taking us all to Hedonism. I have a huge fear of seeing her naked on this beach. That will seriously ruin this whole thing for me." Looking up, he caught site of her and winked. "Speak of the devil."

Molly marched in leading her five bridesmaids behind her.

She looked radiant and his heart melted seeing his sister so happy. She deserved it. Life hadn't been easy for them growing up in a town full of the rich and famous. Their father was lifetime military and although he made good money, he was away more than half the time and their mother had to work like crazy to afford the lifestyle their father had been used to. Molly had missed out on a lot of activities until he was old enough to get a job. He paid for cheerleading uniforms and camp and sent money to her to help with college when he was overseas. She had grown into such a beautiful woman and her job gave her the opportunity to live the life she deserved. Now she was marrying his best friend. He had no doubt Rich would always take care of her. He had been in love with her since the eighth grade and it took him until his junior year in high school to tell her. She was a cute and bubbly sophomore and he had been floored by the declaration. She was safe. Mark smiled. He had done his job.

His eyes returned to his laptop, frantically typing emails to his brokers to make sure everything ran smoothly for the five days he would be gone. The sooner this vacation started, the better. He didn't notice as the passengers begin boarding and taking their seats. The stewardess had taken notice of him however. She had been over to him four times since he sat down offering him a drink or snacks and asking where he would be staying on the island.

"You've always been a good friend to have man," Chad started laughing. "I wouldn't have married Jules if you hadn't been out with me that night. They wouldn't have even noticed me. But you, man, you've still got it. And now I will be supplied with beverages for this extremely long flight."

"I'm going to have to agree with that." The voice came from across the aisle.

Mark looked up and smiled at Caleb and froze. Sitting directly across from him was the very shy little Sophie. He hadn't noticed her sit down but now he couldn't tear his eyes away from her. She had busied herself reading a book and didn't even look up.

Molly had dressed her bridesmaids in pink sweat suits and had worn matching white one. The word bride was written in rhinestones across her back. He looked around at the sea of pink in first class. The girls were all in fitted outfits and were taking off jackets to reveal even tighter white tank tops. But, not Sophie; hers seemed about two sizes too big and she was perfectly content staying covered up.

Sensing his stare, she looked up and their eyes locked. Her blush reached her cheeks before she even had a chance to smile. "Hi"

Mark didn't say a word but didn't stop looking at her. What was wrong with him? On the agenda tonight was find a willing woman on this little Island and work whatever this was out of his system. When her eyes returned to her book, he looked around the cabin again. He had slept with half the bridesmaids and wasn't one to go back for seconds. He shifted in his seat, shut the lap top and closed his eyes. "Screw it! Work will be there when I get home."

****

"Holy shit. What are you reading?" Caleb leaned over and looked at Sophie's book. She immediately started laughing. He tried to take the book from her.

"Take it and die" Sophie squealed. She yanked it back causing Caleb to slam into her.

"No one comes between me and my man."

Mark's eyes shot open. He looked across the aisle to see a cozy Caleb and Sophie now sharing the book. They were both biting their bottom lips. His shoulders instantly stiffened as he glared across the aisle.

"What is that?" He voice was more demanding than he expected but neither of them looked at him. He reached across the aisle and brushed her arm. She jumped and looked over at him with a surprised look.

Chad leaned over and laughed. "That's the book series my wife read a few months ago. That thing is porn without pictures man. My sex life sky rocketed after she read that thing."

Caleb smiled. "First thing I am doing when we check in is taking a cold shower." He tried to steal the book again and Sophie launched herself at him ripping herself from Mark's grip. "Soph, you can't read this stuff. It will ruin you for me."

"Man up Caleb" Ryan yelled from two rows back. "May finally get you laid. I'm tired of hearing Sophie this and Sophie that. Ask her out already."

Caleb froze. Sophie was half across his lap reaching for the book. Her eyes met his and he looked like he was going to pass out. He slumped down in his seat. "Really?" She asked.

Their conversation became whispered and Mark struggled to hear what was being said. He ran his hand down his face and stood up to stretch. She's just a conquest, he reminded himself. That's the only reason you want her. His eyes locked on the stewardess and for a minute he considered taking her into the bathroom. He stepped into the aisle but something stopped him. Sophie chose that exact moment to stand up and tripped over her pant leg. She fell into him and he wrapped his arms around her.

"Always running into me. Keep doing it and I am going to start thinking it's on purpose" Mark laughed as he helped her straightened up.

"I'm sorry" She stuttered. "I just got really hot. I have to get this jacket off and the zipper is stuck."

"Well, it's about five sizes too big Sophie. It's amazing it hasn't fallen off." Mark helped dislodge the zipper and unzipped her jacket. His pants became a little tighter. Her white tank top was exactly the right size. It clung tightly to her perfectly rounded breasts and flat stomach. His brain screamed to touch her.

"Well, it was Natalia's. You should have seen how big the dress was. I didn't get added to this thing until a few days ago." She blushed as he let her go. A visible shiver ran down her spine and he swore her nipples hardened. She looked up at him through her dark lashes and he was instantly hard.

Mark shot away from her and down the aisle away leaving the group behind. He had to get his head right. This was not him. He wanted to pick Caleb up by the neck and remove him from the seat. He, Caleb and Rich had been The Three Musketeers growing up and this was not a thought he had ever had about his best friend before. He knew he and Sophie were friends and worked together but suddenly, that was not OK with him.

****

His smile had been all it took to convince the stewardess in the back that he needed to pace for a few minutes. When she asked if he was nervous about flying he just agreed and she let him blow off some steam as she readied the drink cart for coach.

"Markie?" Molly's voice was quiet and concerned. His eyes met hers but he couldn't stop pacing. "What's happening? You've been gone for a half hour. I'm worried." She put her hands on his arms and he stilled. "Is it the flight? Have you flown since…." Her voice trailed off. She knew he had been through some things during the war but he never talked about it.

"No baby. It's not the flight." He grabbed her and held onto her. His grip tightened as she tried to back up. "I don't know what's happening to me."

"You're soaking wet. What's wrong?" Molly's voice shook.

"I don't know. Everything is closing in on me and I can't breathe." Mark took the drink the stewardess handed him. He was on his third crown and soda. He felt nothing but fear. He chugged the drink and handed it back to the stewardess asking for another. She winked at him but he hardly noticed.

"How many drinks have you had?" Molly leveled her eyes at the stewardess. He just shrugged. "Last one. Chug it down and let's move. Half our crew is asleep and I'm bored. Ryan is being his usual ass self and he and Claire have been practically screwing in full view. I need you up there."

She took his hand and led him slowly through coach until they reached the first class curtain. He took a deep breath and steadied himself. He surveyed the cabin. Rich was asleep against the window, and so were Liz, Amber and Steve. He refused to look at Sophie and Caleb. He sat down next to Chad who just nodded and went back to his magazine. He settled into his seat and took a second deep breath. His curiosity got the best of him and he dared a quick glance at Sophie. She was asleep with her chair reclined. Caleb was looking out the window drumming his fingers on his knee. He couldn't help but notice Sophie's arm still holding the book and resting across Caleb's chest.

****

Arriving at the hotel was total commotion. The lobby was packed and Molly and Rich were being very patient getting the six rooms they had booked.

The wedding party sat clumped together on a large couch waiting for room assignments. It had been a long travel day and the night air felt good against their jetlagged bodies.

"OK. Here's the deal," Rich looked nervous. "The rooms are fine. All six are on the same floor, really close together. Ryan and Claire have asked to room together. I will be with Molls, Obviously Amber and Steve. Liz has asked to bunk with Jessica since she had to leave the hubby at home." He fidgeted. "So. one of you guys is going to have to bunk with Sophie. And Chad, I have gotten death threats from your wife so it won't be you."

"I'll stay with Soph" Caleb perked up and practically yelled.

Molly gave Sophie a sympathetic look and whispered "Is that ok?" Sophie shook her head that is was.

"Here's your key Marco," Rich handed him the same key he had handed Chad. Mark stood there shocked. "Caleb and Sophie are sharing a room?" He said puzzled as he dropped his luggage and fell back onto the couch. He was going to need some more to drink. He was going to need some female companionship. His eyes met Molly's and Molly's jaw dropped.

Chapter 3

She needed to take a walk. Caleb had been great offering to stay with her. After all, he was one of her closest friends in LA and technically her boss, since his senior editor position was the one she worked under. But since the incident on the plane, she had become a little fidgety sharing a room with someone she now saw as a man and not just her friend. He liked her. Not only liked her, he had talked to his friends about her.

Caleb was unpacking quietly. He had let her take the bed by the window so she would have the ocean view in the morning. He was doing everything right. She knew he was attractive. He spent a good amount of time at the gym with Ryan and his body clearly showed that. His smile lit up a room when he walked in and he had more than his share of looks when they went out together. His dirty blond hair, green eyes and little scattering of freckles attracted women wherever they went. But her boyfriend? She closed her eyes and took a deep breath to try to picture herself in his arms. She loved him. But she loved him like her good friend and she couldn't imagine taking it past that point.

He took his t-shirt off and threw it back into his empty suitcase. His body was ripped and Sophie waited to feel something as she watched his strong muscles relax as he stretched. She cleared her throat. "I am going to go for a walk on the beach. Just clear my head a little."

"Want some company?" Caleb grinned and bent to pick up his t-shirt.

"Actually, I would love to just be alone. You've been great. It's just been a long day and I need to just get out there and feel the sand under my feet and feel the breeze hit my face. Is that ok?" She straightened up her pajama pants and tank top and grabbed her flip flops. "I should have packed another sweatshirt. It's breezy out there." She grabbed her keycard and headed for the door.

"Soph?" Caleb threw her his UCLA sweatshirt. She knew it would swallow her but she put it on anyway and headed for the beach.

****

The breeze coming off the ocean was chilly. Mark shivered as he dug his toes further beneath the sand trying to warm his feet. The sounds of the late night party were drowned out by the waves hitting the shore and for the first time all day, he felt at peace.

His dark hair was tussled from trying to sleep and forget. His khaki pants were wrinkled and his white shirt unbuttoned. He rubbed his hands down his face and felt the stubble. It had been a long day. He leaned back onto his elbows and shut his eyes to feel the breeze on his face. This was pure heaven. He knew tomorrow would be crazy with activities, but tonight, this little corner of the beach belonged to him. He started to doze off.

"Hey stranger" The voice was sweet and for a minute he thought he might be dreaming. He opened his eyes slowly and saw her. His body instantly responded. Sitting up he smiled, "Hey yourself." His mind raced.

"Mind if I sit? I think I have walked almost the whole beach. I could use a break."

Gesturing to the sand next to him, Mark took a deep breath to steady himself. "I could use the company. What brings you out here this late?"

She played with a string hanging from the oversized sweatshirt. He recognized it right away. Caleb had worn that sweatshirt every Sunday when they were in college and were looking for a pick up game; Seeing her in it made his chest constrict. "I just needed some air and some distance. It was a really long day." Sophie sighed.

Mark watched as the waves hit the shore and said nothing. The silence was wonderful. He had never met someone that he could just be quiet with. She dug her toes under the sand trying to warm up and just stared into the vast darkness of the ocean. He had to ask. He couldn't let it go any longer. "So, you and Caleb huh?"

Her head snapped toward him. "Me and Caleb what?" She shivered.

"You and Caleb as in You with Caleb. He's a good guy. I've known him since I was five." His stare remained fixed on the darkness.

"No" was all she could manage to say. Was he jealous? She grinned. Being this close to him made her crazy. Even all those years spent with Shawn, she never wanted him the way she wanted Mark. Mark was strong and fit and popular. He was stunning and so far out of her league. Men that looked like him never even spoke to her, let alone let her touch them. But in that moment, she wanted to reach out and touch that rock hard stomach that was showing through his open shirt. His eyes bore into her and after taking a steadying breath, she met his gaze.

"No? You are wearing his clothes and sleeping in his bed. And he has a major thing for you, as pointed out so quietly by my favorite pain in the ass. So, are you sure no?"

"We have two beds. And I am positive. I adore him. He's one of my best friends. But I just don't feel it with him."

"It? I don't know what that is." Mark kept his stare steady and even in the darkness, he could see her blush.

"It. The shivers and the butterflies and the jealousy when other girls look at him. I don't feel it. I mean, he's great. He really is. There's just….." her voiced trailed off as she looked back out at the ocean. She waited a few moments before answering. "Nothing."

"So, is there someone you feel it for?" Mark just kept staring. What was he doing? He wanted to take her right there on the beach. Quiet little covered up Sophie had done something to him and he couldn't understand any of it.

She continued to bother the string hanging from the sweatshirt. Mark had to touch her. He reached out and stopped her hands. He wrapped the loose string around his fingers and pulled it off the sweatshirt. No more interruptions, he told himself. Turning toward her, he gently rolled the sweatshirt sleeves up enough that her hands were free. His whole body screamed at him to kiss her. She nibbled at her bottom lip and her eyes followed his hands, up his arms and stopped when her eyes met his.

He put his hand up to brush her hair behind her ear but stopped himself. He was a one nighter. Sophie deserved so much better. He had one type; easy and hot. This girl didn't seem like either. She was pretty but always so covered up and her shy blush told him there was no way she was easy. He liked to fuck. He didn't snuggle or hold a woman. And only a few occasions had he fallen asleep after and spent the night. He wasn't going to change and he didn't know Sophie well, but he could tell she deserved everything. "Let's walk. I'll walk you back. It's getting late." Mark got to his feet and extended his hand to help her up. When her hand touched his, his body instantly tensed.

What was this woman doing to him?

"So tell me about the infamous Sophie. Where are you from? How did you meet Molls? Is your boyfriend upset you are out here with our crazy bunch?" Mark walked slowly next to her, periodically brushing her arm as they walked.

Sophie just laughed. It was such a beautiful sound. "No boyfriend waiting anywhere. I was engaged but it's a long story. He liked secretaries more than he liked me. We went to college in Georgia and after graduation, I moved to LA with him so he could pursue his music career. Your sister saved me from all that. I was a mess. But she's awesome and kicked my ass into gear. She has the office just outside my lovely cubicle at work. So, other than Molly and Caleb, and the occasional run in with Ryan, that about sums up my social life."

"Do you regret the move?" The conversation with her just flowed and he loved that.

"No. No regrets about the move. I love my job and my tiny apartment. I regret putting all my life into Shawn. But I suppose it taught me what I don't want. Although, no offense to you, men in general are dogs, so it will be a long time before I get involved with someone without really trusting them." She looked at him and smiled. "What about you? Where is Mrs. Moretti? What do you do? Molly told me she had a brother but I know you don't live in LA."

"Actually, I do as of a few days ago. The investment company I work for promoted me so I moved back. I was out in North Carolina after my last tour with the Marines so I stayed and took the first broker job I could find. So, now Molls is stuck with me. I am looking for a house so I am living with Rich at the moment." He stopped walking and wrapped his pinkie around hers. She stopped and looked at him with a small smile on her face. "No Mrs. Moretti. I'm kind of an asshole. I don't think there is someone out there for everyone. Molly says it's just because I won't slow down long enough to open up to anyone. I am just sticking with I'm an asshole."

"Well, it sure seems like you just opened up." Sophie smiled as she walked away from him toward the hotel.

****

Caleb was pacing when she came into the room. He stopped and stared when she opened the door. "You've been gone an hour. I was getting worried. What's with the grin?"

Sophie kicked off her shoes and laughed. "Always my protector, aren't you? Relax, I'm back. I'm fine. I ran into Mark and we talked for awhile and he walked me back."

Caleb threw himself across the bed. "No Sophie, absolutely not."

She took off his sweatshirt and shook some of the sand out of it. "No what? What are you talking about? God, I got a lot of sand in your sweatshirt. I'm sorry."

Caleb shot off the bed and grabbed her arm. "Did you do something with him?"

"Hey" she yanked out of his grasp. "No, of course not. I just met the guy three days ago. Please tell me you know me better than that."

"I'm sorry. He's just not good for you. He's a loner. And he sleeps with everything that moves. But he only does it once. He will never be able to love you. He loves himself and his perfect car and perfect job but will never love a woman. And that's just who he is.

Don't let him lure you in Soph. He's just looking for his next conquest and you are the only one that he hasn't slept with in the whole bridal party."

"Well," She smiled and sighed. "He is quite handsome."

"Sophie, he will crush you. He will crush you and never even look back and all of us will have to pick up the pieces. He's a dog."

"Caleb Allen!! How can you talk about him like that? He said you were his best friend." Sophie glared at him. "He told me you were a good guy and that you had been friends since kindergarten. How can you be so mean?"

"Don't defend him. You'll see." Caleb crawled under the

covers. "He may be one of my best friends. But he is who he is Soph."

Sophie crawled under her covers and turned the lights off. "That was really unexpected from you. If that's how you talk about one of your best friends, I would hate to hear how you talk about me."

There was silence for a minute and Caleb cleared his throat. "It's different Soph. I am in love with you."

Chapter 4

Mark felt the sun baking his skin and it was pure heaven. He hadn't been this relaxed for years. Even with all the activity around him, he planned on doing nothing all day but lying in his chair and taking the occasional dip. The drinks were flowing freely and the waitress from the tiki bar on the beach had noticed him right away. He had done his best to flirt but had somehow lost his edge in a mere 24 hours. He could wink, however, and that seemed to keep their drinks coming. Ryan was sitting two chairs down from him and decided that he deserved a little alone time with the waitress. When she realized she was going nowhere with Mark, she turned her attention to Ryan.

"Dude, aren't you already screwing your roommate this trip?" Chad couldn't believe when he heard the waitress ask him to meet her in an hour behind the nightclub.

"It's Hendonism Bro. Get what you can. Your wife will never know. Indulge a little. What happens here is none of anyone's business. Later, we are heading to the nude side and I don't want to hear any protests. We are on vacation."

"You are a pig West. A damn pig." Chad turned his head to Mark. "Look dude, I know you are kind of a man whore and my hero, but you know I can't cheat on my wife."

Mark finally looked at the two. He was having no part in any of their shit. "Thanks for the man whore thing. But even this man whore doesn't think you should cheat on your wife Perry. That would be something you could never take back."

"Who've you been banging Moretti? We've been here 24 hours now. I'm sure your dance cards full if you know what I mean." Ryan surveyed the prospects.

"No one. Not sure I will." Mark put his sunglasses back on and returned to worshipping the sun.

"Come with me. Come to the nightclub. Not like we haven't done that before. She'd love it." Ryan looked at his watch.

"I'm good man, really." He refused to look over at his friend. This was ridiculous.

An offer like that would have had his blood pumping a week ago. He contemplated going. He needed to do something. He was off his game. Not only was he off his game, he wasn't even aware there was a game going on. Something had to give.

"Look who's whipped." Ryan laughed noticing Caleb making his way to join them.

Mark looked behind him. Caleb was balancing a blanket, a book, sunscreen, a beach bag and two drinks. He took a deep breath. This was going to be a long day if he was going to have to watch Caleb get all cozy with Sophie.

"Sophie seems like a nice girl. I think Caleb made a good

choice." Chad took a long swig of beer.

"And she's got a tight ass and some nice tits on her." Ryan looked at Caleb, "Where's your girlfriend? Get any yet?"

Mark shot Ryan the death gaze, "Don't talk about her like that."

"Molly has all the girls up there drinking some sort of shot. They are all sitting around the pool bar wearing the equivalent of floss for bathing suits and the bartender is totally into them. He's just pouring all kinds of liquor down their throats. When some dude did a body shot off Sophie, I had enough. Figure even with West down here, it can't be that bad."

Mark was pissed. There was no other way to describe it. His

blood boiled. The thought of someone touching Sophie had him wound so tight he could kill someone. He waved the waitress over and ordered a double round of shots. He would drink and doze off under the sun's rays and forget because if he walked to the pool, someone was dead.

****

"I certainly didn't think I would end up sharing my book with you this vacation," Molly tugged the book back away from Caleb and giggled.

"I didn't think I could get so turned on reading something like this. I swear Soph, I don't know how you are not nuts right now." Caleb grabbed the suntan lotion. "I have to put this on your back. I'm sorry but I have to touch you. Right now!"

That got Mark's attention. For the past half hour he had resisted the urge to look over at them. Even asleep, his body was aware when Sophie joined them. He kept his eyes glued shut, not daring to look at her in her bathing suit. If it was anything like he was picturing in his mind, he would be hard in a second. His body was at war with itself. His brain told him he was no good and he needed to stay away but the rest of his body screamed that it had to have her. He knew that couldn't happen. He knew that it could ruin everything and the wedding and Molly's happiness needed to remain his number one priority.

"Oh My God!" They said in Unison. Sophie flattened herself against the blanket and buried her face into her towel. Caleb leaned in and whispered something to her but she pushed him away playfully. She giggled but kept her red face buried in the towel. Caleb shifted his swim trunks.

"Legs," he said breathless. "Your legs need sunscreen." He started applying the sunscreen slowly down her leg, starting dangerously near the edge of her swimsuit. Mark's brain roared.

"Caleb?" Her voice was muffled. She wiggled her finger to draw his attention to her. He plopped down right next to her without even and inch in between them. She whispered so no one else could hear them. "I appreciate the sunscreen. But, it doesn't matter how much sunscreen you apply to any exposed part of my body. We can't do this. And it's the book C. It's just the book. So please, stop looking at me with your eyes half closed and touching me like that. If anything happened between us right now, it would be the book. And that's not fair to you. And it would ruin everything."

Mark smiled. They were sitting close enough to him that he could hear everything. He finally risked a glance their way and instantly regretted it. She was wearing the smallest bathing suit he had ever seen. The pink fabric tied tightly across her back and around her neck. The tiny piece of fabric covering her perfect, round and beautiful ass might as well not even be there. He longed to touch it. He thanked God she hadn't turned over. He could only imagine the shot he would get of those beautiful rounded breasts. His little, covered up Sophie was practically naked. His? When did he start thinking of her as his? His cock strained against his swim trunks. This was bad. She was gorgeous. Band-Aid girl was gorgeous. He couldn't stand it. He had to touch her and he had to touch her now.

He stood up and threw her over his shoulder. She screamed. "That's it bookworm; It's time to go for a dip." She giggled and tried to pull herself up as he ran through the hot sand into the ocean. The water splashed around his legs as he ran deeper.

"Don't you dare drop me, Mark. Don't you dare!" She was laughing so hard she could hardly catch her breath. This was so unexpected. She kicked her legs in protest. "I can't swim."

"Yes you can," Mark laughed with her.

"Um.. I have my contacts in. I can't get my hair wet. I am allergic to…" Her sentence was cut off as he flung her back first into the deeper water. She broke the surface laughing and trying to pull back the hair that was in her face. She saw him dive under the water and swim for her legs. She squealed and tried to run. He surfaced right next to her and splashed her.

Mark was laughing as he tried to get away from her. He knew payback would be a bitch but he knew he could move faster than she could. She was shoulder deep and the water barely hit his chest.

"Mark Moretti, you get your ass back here right now." She splashed large waves of water at him as she ran to catch up. He taunted her and splashed her back. He was heading to deeper water and she could no longer touch. She swam after him and when she finally caught up with him, she jumped onto his back. "I can't touch." She was out of breath and her panting hit him in the back of the neck sending goose bumps down his arms.

"Looks like you need me now, huh?" Mark laughed and threw

her off his shoulder. As she surfaced, she laughed and cupped her hands to splash him. He reached out and grabbed her arms and pulled her back against him. He instantly hardened and her body went rigid in his arms. He froze. Oh God she knew.

She relaxed back into him and rubbed that perfect ass against his erection. She moaned softly and rubbed again. Mark growled low in his throat as he tightened his grip around her waist. He turned his back to shore to block what was happening. When she moaned again and rubbed against him a third time, he whimpered. "God, Sophie. You make me so crazy. You are beautiful."

"I want to turn around," she said breathlessly.

"You can't Soph. You can't. I won't be able to stop myself if you do." He kissed behind her ear and nibbled on her ear lobe. "You have been drinking. This isn't you. And I won't stop. God please don't turn around."

"Please Mark, please touch me" she whimpered as he ran his hand up her flat stomach to her breast. Her nipple hardened and he ran his fingers over it. "More."

Mark looked to his sides to make sure no one was watching and slipped his fingers under the flimsy fabric covering her breasts. He pinched her right nipple and she arched back into his erection. She was panting. "I'm gonna turn around."

His hands tightened around her. "Sophie, if you turn around, I'm going to lose it. I won't be able to help myself. I'm not good for you. You deserve more and if you turn around, I'm afraid you're going to regret it. I won't be able to stop. I can't hurt you like that." He was panting and shaking. He leaned in to kiss her neck and she turned her head into him. Her lips met his and her tongue begged for entrance. When his lips parted, her tongue wrestled with his. She moaned into his mouth and his erection grew painfully larger.

Her hands roamed backwards until they found his erection and his body froze. She fumbled with the tie of his swim trunks and moaned in frustration when she couldn't get it untied. She rubbed her hand over his shorts the entire length of him. His grip loosened as he threw his head back. She turned and his breath hitched when she wrapped her legs around him.

"Sophie," his breathing was erratic. Her eyes met his and she melted. She wrapped her arms around him and ground into his erection. His eyes snapped shut. "Oh God Sophie. What are you doing?"

"Look at me, Mark." She panted. He opened his eyes and met hers. "Touch me. Please touch me." She ground against him a few more times.

His vision went blurry. He pushed her bathing suit bottoms over and ran his fingers through her folds. Even in the water, he could tell she was soaking wet.

He moaned. "Holy shit, you are so wet. I am not going to be able stop. You need to stop this Soph because I can't. No Sex. We can't. You deserve more than this." His words were strained and breathless.

She leaned forward and sucked the salty water off his chest and licked up his neck. "I won't regret this. I want you so bad." She smiled with her eyes half closed. "Touch me."

Mark shoved a finger into her core and flicked the pad of his thumb against her swollen clit. She threw her head back and moaned. A second finger and a second flick and her head crashed against his chest panting. "Don't stop." His fingers furiously pounded into her as she tried again to untie his shorts. The knot loosened and she slipped his shorts down lower on his hips. His thumb continued to circle her clit and she began nibbling at his neck. "Come for me baby. Let it go." Marks voice was raspy and full of sex. Her orgasm hit her so hard that she had to collapse against him to keep from sliding under the water. He wrapped his arm under her bottom and pulled her against him. "Watching your face was the most beautiful thing I have ever seen." Mark kissed her hard and she frantically tried to free his erection. "Sophie, don't. We can't go this far."

"I've wanted you from the second I saw you. I don't want to stop." Sophie grasped his erection and stroked it once, twice. Mark became crazed. She slid her bikini bottoms over and poised herself over the tip of his erection. His knees went weak.

"Oh God Soph. Are you sure?" He could hardly keep himself together. He pulled her back and looked into her eyes. His arms tightened to keep her at a distance, just hovering over the head of his erection. "We can't take this back. You know the kind of guy I am."

"You don't want me?" She tried to wiggle free; her slick core resting on the head of his cock. She ground against the tip and his eyes slammed shut.

"I have never wanted anyone like I want you." His expression was pained as he tried to control his breathing. "You do something to me Sophie. I just don't understand it." As she stroked her body lightly over the head he almost cried out in frustration.

She whimpered and tried to break free of his death grip. She wanted all of him. She wanted him right now. She had never acted like this but Mark made her crazed. When she realized he wouldn't loosen his grip, she reached down between them and stroked him with her hand. Her lips met his and he was lost.

"Oh God Soph," he let her go. "I can't hold back any longer. Just do it."

She crawled up his body once more and wrapped her legs tightly around his waist. He was so hard. And it was all for her. She grabbed his erection and positioned herself over the tip. This was it. She was so ready for him. He could feel the heat from her and he moaned.

"Guys!!!" Rich yelled from the beach and they both froze. "Come on. Lunch is served. We're all up there waiting for you. Let's go."

Chapter 5

Sophie swam to shore scanning the line of empty towels that had been occupied by her group. She could not believe what she had just done. Not only had she almost had sex with Mark Moretti, she had initiated it and had potentially put on a show for her whole group. It was like doing the walk of shame when she exited the water into Rich's arms. He held the towel around her shoulders and gave her a little chuckle. "Don't worry Soph. Ryan had gone to meet some waitress and the girls had gone back to the pool. Chad went to call his wife so no one saw that."

"Caleb?" Her voice cracked and she hid her face against towel.

"No. Ryan had bet him a hundred bucks he couldn't get a girl's number so he walked off once you went into the water." He started laughing. "Sorry I interrupted Soph. Go join everyone at lunch and I will wait here for Marco."

Sophie looked back at Mark as he made his way to shore. He was staring at her, his eyes burning into her. She bit her bottom lip and Rich just laughed. "You need to put something on."

Sophie jumped away from him and looked down and didn't notice anything out of place. "Why? What's wrong?"

"You are driving that boy of ours mad. He's been wound tight since the first time he saw you. Just cover up and let's make it through lunch. The only other thing on the agenda today is snorkeling at 3:00 so the rest of the time is all yours."

Sophie looked over at her towel. She hadn't worn anything down to the beach but her bikini. She noticed Caleb's shirt lying on the blanket and grabbed it. Throwing it on, she jogged to the dinning room.

"Get that out of your system yet Marco?" Rich just laughed as Mark adjusted the tie at his waistband. "Can we get on with our trip now?"

"Shit man. Perfect timing," he gave Rich the death stare. "What the fuck is wrong with me?"

Putting his arm around him, Rich led him up to the restaurant. "You know, the first time I saw your sister, I knew. I loved her the second she looked at me."

"Dude that was middle school bullshit; I'm not capable of that emotion." Mark rubbed his hand down the front of his face and then straightened up.

Rich just shook his head. "You love Molly. You'd take a bullet for her. Why couldn't you love someone else like that?"

Mark was completely silent when they joined the rest of the group. Molly looked up concerned and patted the seat next to her. "You OK?" she whispered.

"No," Mark put his napkin into his lap and took a sip of water.

Molly leaned in and kissed his shoulder. "What's the matter?" When Mark didn't answer her, she took his hand under the table. He was trembling. "What is wrong Markie? You are scaring me." Her voice was quiet but shook asking the question.

"Molls, drop it. I'll be fine." He took another sip of water and glanced across the table in time to see Caleb drop down in the seat next to Sophie. His whole face hardened in anger.

"I don't know what it is Soph, but you sure know how to make my blood boil. You look sexy in my clothes baby." Caleb spoke a little too loud and everyone looked up. Sophie just blushed and kept her gaze fixed on her salad plate. He reached out and tucked her hair behind her ear and kissed her forehead.

Mark saw red. His hand squeezed Molly's until his knuckles were white. Molly hissed in a breath and looked at him.

Ryan came stumbling into the room laughing. He was drunk and sweating. "Marco, Dude!" He came over and high fived a fuming Mark. "She's waiting for you. She's ready bro and she is hot!"

The whole group started in on how rude Ryan was. Everyone except for Caleb. He leaned in and gave Sophie a kiss on the neck and whispered something into her ear.

Mark pounded his fist on the table and everyone jumped. He shoved his chair back and stormed out of the dining room.

"Oh Yeah," Ryan slurred. "Marco's got his groove back."

Sophie sat there with her jaw dropped as Mark walked away from the table.

****

Mark stood under the cold water as it pelted his shoulders. He could still hear Sophie's little moans and smell her sweet Jasmine smell. Her taste was still in his mouth and his mind raced. Remnants of their time in the ocean were all over him. It had almost been heaven. There was no other word that described what she would have felt like. His whole body ached for her. His hand slapped against the tiled side of the shower and he threw his head back. This wouldn't take long. He roared her name as the pain and pleasure of the morning crashed around him.

****

Sophie lay sobbing into her pillow when the bedroom door opened. Caleb dropped everything in his hands and ran over to her. He lay down next to her and pulled her into his arms. She was trembling and the tears flooded her face. "Shhhh. Soph, it's ok. I'm here. What happened baby?"

She shifted her body into his and buried her face into his neck. Her sobs were uncontrollable and for a long time, he just stroked her hair and held her. When she began to settle down, he asked her again. "What happened?"

She pulled back and looked at him and then sat up. "I didn't listen to you. I should have. I didn't." She started crying again.

"What are you talking about?" Caleb looked puzzled and held his hands out to her. The thought hit him like a ton of bricks. "Mark. You lied to me about Mark last night." His voice got louder.

"No, No I didn't." Sophie said backing away from him. "It was this morning."

Caleb stood up and crossed the room. "What did he do to you Soph?" When she didn't answer immediately, he asked louder. "What. Did. He. Do. To. You?" Each word was clipped and made her cringe.

"He didn't do it. I did." Sophie threw her hands to her face and continued sobbing.

"I don't understand." Caleb's eyes filled with tears. "What do you mean you did?"

"Caleb, I have wanted him since the engagement party. I can't breathe when he's near me. I couldn't help it."

Caleb backed all the way up to the door shaking his head. "This cannot be happening. Are you kidding me?"

"Stop yelling at me!" Sophie snapped at him

"Where was I?" A tear ran down Caleb's face and he yelled at her. "Where was I? I have been with you this whole trip."

"You were on the beach." It broke Sophie's heart to see Caleb cry. She knew he had tried to warn her. She hadn't cared.

"In the water?" Caleb was yelling. "What the hell Sophie? I was right there. I watched you guys splashing each other. I was jealous as hell. And the whole time you were planning on fucking him? In front of me?"

"I wasn't planning it. It happened. Well, it didn't. But it almost did. And then he…"

"It did or it didn't Sophie?" Caleb pushed his head back against the door. The room was spinning and he couldn't catch his breath.

'It didn't. But I wanted it to." Sophie stood staring at him. She was shocked to see his reaction. She needed him to comfort her. Mark had left lunch right after Ryan came back and told him it was his turn. Her heart had shattered into a million pieces and she watched him walk toward the waitress. She needed her best friend.

"God Damnit Sophie. I told you I loved you. How could you do this?" He reached for the door knob…

****

Mark made his way down the hall feeling so much better. He knew he would have to endure a few hours on a boat with her this afternoon but he had cleared his head. Love. He laughed. No way. Rich didn't know what he was talking about. He didn't even know her. He heard the yelling before he got to the door. Muffled sounds from a woman and Caleb's voice clear as day.

"It did or it didn't Sophie?" Mark stopped outside the door and took a step toward it. A muffled female voice responded and there was a thud at the door. "God damnit Sophie. I told you I loved you. How could you do this?"

The hair on the back of Mark's neck stood up. He raised a fist to knock on the door when it flew open. Caleb was red faced and his eyes were puffy. He was furious. "Perfect timing Moretti! You can twist the knife that was just shoved in my back." He stormed past him down the hall.

Mark looked into the room and saw Sophie curled into a ball on the bed sobbing. He stepped in. "Sophie?"

"Get out Mark!" Her voice was strong despite the tears.

He walked over to her and touched her. She looked him right in the eye and he swore he saw hatred. "You all nice and clean and showered? You feel better?" She spat at him.

He put his hands in his pockets and crouched down near her. "Sophie," his hand reached out and stroked her cheek and she sobbed. "Baby, what happened?" He froze. Baby? He knew there were more cold showers on the horizon.

"Get. Out!" Sophie shoved him back and he lost his balance. When he stood up and looked at her, his heart broke.

"What did he do to you Sophie?" Mark's anger flared.

"What did HE do to me? Ha! That's classic. What did YOU do to me? Get out!" Sophie stood up and shoved him out the door and slammed it in his face.

Chapter 6

This was exactly why Mark didn't date. Drama. Plain and simple. He had no idea what was happening but his best friend was hurting and pissed at the girl that he couldn't get out of his mind. He knew nothing about their argument and decided it was best if it stayed that way. What he did know for sure was this snorkeling trip was really going to suck.

"Marco!" Ryan yelled from the bar, waving him over to sit with him. The waitress was currently tending bar and she smiled at Mark when he walked up.

"What can I get you handsome?"

She was still trying. Mark groaned. "Give me something strong that's gonna put me on my ass. Then, make it a double please." He put his head into his hands and groaned.

Ryan laughed, "Trouble in paradise my friend?" He leaned forward and pinched the bartender's ass and she squealed. "I thought this afternoon that you were heading to tap that fine ass right there. But when I found her alone, I had to take care of it again myself. Where did you go?"

"I had something else I had to take care of. I'm kind of trying to stay away from the whole screw everything that moves image." Even before the words came out of his mouth, he knew he actually meant them. It scared him to death.

"Why?" Ryan looked stunned. "Please tell me the infamous Mark Moretti does not have some girl back in North Carolina because that will seriously ruin my trip."

Mark took a long chug of what tasted like rubbing alcohol and looked out at the boat that they would be snorkeling from. Caleb was already aboard and for some reason, Mark's anger immediately returned. This was ridiculous. *He's your best friend*, he told himself. Mark took another long chug. "Ugh, what is this?"

"You said you wanted to be drunk. This will do it." Ryan ordered him another and grabbed it before they headed to the boat. "Let's get this shit over with. I got a lot to do when we get back."

"Seriously dude? How many women do you think you have slept with?" Mark took another long chug.

"Today?" Ryan and Mark both laughed as they boarded the boat.

The tension was instant. Ryan looked between Caleb and Mark and took a seat in the middle. Thankfully, Molly and Rich chose that minute to board. Caleb just paced at the front of the boat. Mark contemplated going over and punching him but he didn't know what had gone down between him and Sophie and he thought it would be better to defend her honor when he knew what Caleb had done. He crossed his arms over his chest and sat back.

"Allen, if you are done with your pity party, I need you back here. Let the girls sit up front. I need to talk to you about the bachelor party." Naturally, Ryan had been put in charge of the party that was sure to get them all in trouble. Caleb walked back to them and sat as far from Mark as he could. "So I am thinking Vegas the weekend before the wedding. A buddy I train has a sweat pad up there and we could stay there. You know what they say about Vegas."

"Guys, I'm sorry," Rich interrupted. "I really don't want a bachelor party. I know it's tradition. But that's kind of why we wanted you all here.

We just wanted some time away. I don't need another weekend right away. We can always do a guys weekend but I don't need that."

"Bullshit." Ryan took a sip of Mark's drink and gagged. "You are the groom. Last weekend of freedom and all that."

One by one the rest of the wedding party boarded the boat. Sophie was last and stepped aboard in a lace bathing suit cover up. She wore large sunglasses but her cheeks were still flushed and puffy. She walked past the men to the front of the boat and sat down next to Amber. Mark watched her. She moved so gracefully. Her blond hair was swept up in a loose braid and she had changed into a black bikini.

She had gotten some sun today and looked stunning. He smiled at her when he thought she was looking but the smile wasn't returned. Amber whispered something to her and when Sophie sighed a tear escaped down her cheek. Amber listened to the whole story, nodding her head and patting her leg. Having Amber sit so close to Sophie worried him since he had slept with Amber only six nights ago. But that was before he met Sophie. That was before his heart started to betray him.

****

Molly floated along the surface looking down at the most amazing coral and fish she had ever seen. She occasionally glanced back up at the boat to check on her brother. He was passed out on his stomach, getting the late afternoon sun on his back. Ryan had told them that they had hit the bar and he had a few drinks that could take down an elephant. "I'm worried about him."

"He's fine Molly. He's been through some shit. You have to just give him some time. You know he saw a lot of crazy stuff over there. I know he's been back awhile but sometimes it just takes some time to get your head right." Ryan swam between Molly and Amber, glancing at Amber's ass more than at the fish. "He has to get back out there. Man up. He'll be fine. I think he might have met someone."

"He's already manned up," Molly glared at Amber. "And he's not fine. He's wound tight.

And honestly, I think it has something to do with Sophie. Does that sound crazy?"

"Molls, your brother is never going to settle down if that's what you're hoping for. I don't care what he's thinking right now. He's been my wing man way too long. No way. He's a player for life." Ryan reached out and touched Amber's ass.

"Seriously dude?" Caleb swam up beside them.

"Oh, thank God someone honest. What's wrong with Mark?" Molly swam over to Caleb and held onto his strong arms as they treaded water. "It has to do with Sophie, doesn't it?" Caleb groaned. "I know you have feelings for her. I'm so sorry. But I am worried about Mark. He's been angry and standoffish and now he's drunk. Please C. Please tell me what you know. Ryan thinks he met someone. That's crazy, right?"

"Molls, I love you. But I think you need to ask him what's happening with him. All I will say is that I am in love with Sophie but she has feelings for someone on this trip and it's damn sure not me."

"Five More Minutes" the boat captain yelled. Mark startled awake and sat up.

He looked around at his group of friends. He had to get his head on straight because he was ruining this trip for his sister and Rich. He had been away from them for so long and this was his homecoming. He couldn't blow it. He needed some clarity on the Sophie front and he would get it as soon as he could. He scanned the water and saw her swimming with Chad. They were smiling and laughing and Chad was telling her horror stories about sharks with giant teeth. She was happy and he was glad. The rest of the group was scattered in different areas around the boat. He smiled. This was his family and it was time he started acting like it.

"Come here you idiot." Amber yanked Caleb toward her. "Do you know what you did to her today?"

"Ha. What I did?" Caleb tried to push away.

"She was totally played. She has feelings for this guy who practically screws her and then leaves from lunch to have sex with the waitress from the bar this morning. And you yell at her?" Amber smacked at his chest and pointed at Sophie and Chad getting out of the water. "You yelled at her and she needed you. Well played Caleb, well played."

Caleb was swimming to the boat before Amber could finish. He felt like such an asshole. He thought she was upset because she had fallen for the guy and didn't want to tell him. He let his emotions take over and had been so angry. And all afternoon he had ignored her like she was nothing. She was everything to him. And even if she couldn't return his feelings, she was his friend and no one could take her place. He was such a fool.

He rocketed onto the boat, dropping his fins into the crate and pushing past everyone. He knelt in front of Sophie and took her hands in his. "Look at me." She wouldn't look up. He gently grabbed her chin and forced her to make eye contact with him. "Soph, I am so sorry. I am so so sorry. I didn't know. I didn't know what he did."

She launched herself forward into his arms and cried. He held her as she trembled and whispered that it would be ok. He ran his fingers down her braid and kissed her softly on the shoulder. "You needed me and I turned on you. I won't do that again Soph. No matter what, I love you and I will always be there for you." He stood up and sat down with her on his lap. She traced his Celtic arm band tattoo and began to calm down. "He's my best friend Soph. He always has been. I won't take sides in this. But I will be here when you need me because falling for someone that doesn't love you back really sucks."

"Enough!" Mark jumped out of his seat as the boat started speeding away. He tried to walk to the front of the boat but Amber stopped him.

"Don't you dare go up there! Haven't you done enough for today? Don't you hurt her anymore." Amber grabbed his arm and shoved him. Her screaming got everyone's attention.

"Whoa, what the hell Amber?" Rich stood up and grabbed her.

"Ask this asshole. Leading Sophie on and then going to get laid by some waitress. Solid guy. She fell for this asshole. She doesn't need anymore of his shit today."

Ryan looked up. "Mark didn't sleep with Tabitha. That was me." He looked confused.

"Bullshit. He left the table and met up with her after lunch. You walked in and said she was waiting for him. He got right up and went to her." Everyone was looking at her as she kept trying to shove Mark. Sophie cuddled closer to Caleb and whimpered.

"I NEVER slept with her." Mark looked Sophie right in the eye. "I didn't go anywhere near her. I went up to my room and took a damn cold shower."

"He's telling the truth. I went back to where I left Tabitha and she was still there waiting on him but he never showed." Ryan was a player but he always had someone's back in a fight.

"You mean to tell me you passed up a free piece of Ass Moretti? I highly doubt it." Amber huffed as she sat back down.

"Nothing is ever free Amber! What right do you have to get in my face? Hi pot. I'm Kettle." He shook her hand and seethed as he looked at her, "And, yes, even a man whore like me can pass up a piece of ass."

Mark turned away and went back to his seat at the back of

the boat. There was so much drama over one false piece of information. He looked right at Molly, "This is why I am single; all this shit right here. I spent the day trying to figure out what the hell was happening to me and why Sophie was so upset. But did anyone talk to me? Did anyone ask what the truth might really be? Nope. This is the perfect example of why I always have been and why I always will be solo. Sorry sis."

He pulled his sunglasses up over his eyes and turned his head to watch the scenery as the boat made its final approach to the hotel.

Chapter 7

She'd blown it. Yesterday had been a disaster. Hearing Mark tell everyone on the boat that he hadn't met the waitress and then hearing Ryan defend him was heartbreaking. His face showed complete betrayal by everyone on the boat. And, it was all her fault. She had jumped to conclusions and confided in Amber who just couldn't let it go. And all those faces on the boat, all the people he loved more than anyone in the world, they had all believed her without a second thought. Well, everyone but Rich. He looked just as shocked as Mark and had done his best to convince him to join the group for dinner. But Mark had bowed out, saying he wasn't feeling well. She knew the truth.

"Caleb, are you awake?" She whispered into the dark room as the first streaks of morning sun snuck through the curtain.

"No." He grunted and rolled over. Caleb had been out late with the guys and she knew his head was probably pounding..

"Can you be awake?" Sophie begged in a little girl voice.

"Are you on fire?" Caleb waited for an answer but just heard her huff. "Unless you have a strong urge to seduce me right now, I am going to sleep some more. If you want to seduce me, I will totally be up for that." His voice was groggy but she could tell he was smiling.

Sophie just sighed. She stretched and got up to brush her teeth and hair and then made her way toward the balcony. Opening the blinds just a tiny bit, she looked out at the beautiful sun just making its appearance. The beach was quiet. She felt like it was all hers. She stepped into the fresh air and got comfy in one of the oversized chairs.

There was a small breeze coming off the ocean and she pulled her legs up to wrap her arms around them. This was heaven. The world was at peace in this moment and even with all the thoughts swimming through her head, she was able to take a deep breath and smile. Despite this crazy place, full of parties, nudity and alcohol, she was having a great time. She straightened her pony tail and promised herself that today, she would make things right with Mark and enjoy the last days in paradise.

The wedding party had welcomed her with open arms and she felt like she had been a part of the group forever. Ryan still shocked her with the things he said but she was getting used to him. The few times she had gone with Caleb and Molly to meet Ryan out at a nightclub, she had been hit on relentlessly and Molly had brushed him away each time. Caleb had always just sat by her side, sometimes with his arm around her, to help protect her from Ryan's perverted assaults. He was smoking hot, no doubt about that. But she had never met anyone that went home with someone new every time they went out.

Her life was much more reserved. She'd only had a few boyfriends. She somehow found herself just one of the guys in high school and that continued on to college. Her sister had been the social butterfly, dating and having fun and Sophie just stood in the shadows. Then she met Shawn and life for her changed. She was determined to wait until their wedding night to make love, but he had a different idea and had talked her into it about a year into their relationship. She spent the next three years having periodic sex and really didn't know what the big deal was. It was never great. She never burned for him and was never so turned on she couldn't wait to be with him.

But Mark. She sighed. She knew him all of six days and she would have given herself completely to him in the water yesterday if Rich hadn't interrupted. Just one look into his green eyes and her whole body tingled. His lips on her neck had ignited her blood and she was on fire for him. Feeling his erection against her back had done something to her and her good girl side was completely obliterated. He was sex personified. She ran her fingers over her lips. She could still feel his tongue fighting against hers as he begged her to be good because he couldn't.

The sound of footfalls on the wet sand drew her attention from her fantasy. Her breath hitched. Mark was running the beach. His shoes hit the line where the water and sand met and his footprints were the only ones on the beach. Her breath turned heavy as she watched him. He was wearing black shorts that left little to the imagination. His leg muscles pulsed as he ran. He was wearing his dog tags and they hit his bare chest with each new stride. Sweat poured off his face onto his chest and back. The muscles in his stomach rippled as his strong shoulders and arms pumped. He was beautiful. There was no other way to describe it. She heard Rich call his name but he never looked back. His music blared in his ears. As he reached the fence line, he turned and came back toward the hotel. Rich had walked toward him and when he spotted him, he took his ear buds out and wiped his eyes. When they met, Mark hunched over, hands on his knees, trying to catch his breath. Rich put his had on his back and looked concerned. There was no way he was crying. Was there? Certainly he must have just been wiping sweat. She leaned forward in her seat and strained to hear what they were saying.

****

The beach was his. He had run the whole length of the property more times than he could count. Running was his outlet and he needed to relieve some stress. The tears were a little much but he couldn't stop himself. Everything was crashing down on him at once. He hadn't seen his friends in so long and he couldn't be angry at them for thinking he was the same old Mark. His conquests with Ryan were legendary.

And it certainly didn't help his cause that he had slept with Amber about fifteen minutes into seeing her again. And she was engaged? This was a disaster. His feet pounded harder and he picked up his pace. The old Mark would have gone out and picked up a girl and taken her home, or wherever was closest, and would never have called her again. He knew it seemed cold. But he was upfront with them from the very beginning so he found it difficult to understand when they continued to call him and why they acted heart broken. He was a one night stand. And that's all he'd ever be.

Then he saw clumsy Sophie in the grocery store last week and his heart had leapt into his throat. He had to get away from her right away because when he looked into her eyes, he felt something he had never felt looking at other women. Then in some sick twist of fate, she turned out to be the maid of honor and his sister's best friend. She was off limits. He had promised himself that much. But as soon as they hit that water yesterday and her skin touched his, the walls around his heart shattered. After the disaster otherwise known as snorkeling, he knew what Sophie truly thought of him. So he was done. He was done sulking and done pining after her. It was best this way.

The run had shattered all his stress into a mess of tears he couldn't control. Everything he felt from mourning the loss of his friends during the war, then leaving the Marines, to leaving his new friends to move home to LA, to his baby sister getting married, all seemed to come out at once. He felt so at peace. He was getting rid of years of stress and sadness and he had a feeling it was because Sophie had made him feel something for the first time in forever. Someday he would thank her. But for now, she was off limits.

His eyes caught Rich standing down the beach waving at him. Perfect, he thought. To add insult to injury, his best friend was about to see him cry. This was the least manly thing he had ever done in front of Rich. He removed his ear buds and ran toward him. He grabbed his hips, then his knees trying to catch his breath and control his emotions.

"I thought I might find you out here." Rich put his hand on his back. "You alright buddy? I'm sorry about yesterday. That was some shit."

Mark panted, "It's fine. It's over. I am ready to rejoin you guys today." He stood up and looked Rich in the eyes. "Just needed to get some stuff out of my system."

Rich noticed he had been crying. "Whenever you're ready, I'm here. In the mean time, I would love some company for breakfast if you're up to it."

"Ok," Mark straightened up and turned to the hotel and Rich threw an arm over his shoulder. "Let me grab a quick shower and I'll meet you down here in fifteen."

Mark ran up the steps, burst through the hallway door and smacked right into Sophie. He grabbed her arms to catch her and made sure she was steady. "Sorry Sophie. I wasn't paying any attention. Did I hit you?" He looked her over to make sure she was OK.

"I was actually coming to look for you. I saw you running. I was wondering if we could talk?" Sophie's eyes sparkled up at him and for a moment he was lost. He didn't answer. "Mark?"

He snapped out of his trance and shook his head. "I need some time Sophie." He let go of her arms and made the long trip down the hallway to his room.

****

Time. She gave him all of five minutes before she changed her mind and walked down to his room. She tapped lightly on the door and a minute later was met with Chad's big grin.

"I'm sorry it's so early. I need to talk to Mark." She glanced around the room nervously.

Chad yawned and patted his hair into place. "Caleb still in your room? I'll give you guys some space. Just let me know when it's safe to come back." When Sophie nodded, he grabbed his swim trunks and flip flops and walked out the door.

She could hear the shower running so she sat down on the bed with the running shoes next to it and froze. What if he came out of the bathroom in nothing? What if he was mad? She should have thought this through. Too late. She heard the door click open.

"Hey I'm heading down to….." His voice trailed off as he saw Sophie sitting on his bed. She was still in her pajamas which didn't leave much to the imagination. Her sheer white tank top clung to every inch of her chest and her boxer shorts were so short and loose he could easily.. No. He had to stop thinking like that. "What are you doing here?"

Sophie's jaw dropped when he walked out of the bathroom. He had a towel wrapped loosely over his hips, his dog tags around his neck and absolutely nothing else on. He smelled like soap and mint. She inhaled deeply and her hands shook. His chest was perfect. He was covered in muscle, every inch more impressive than the last. His broad shoulders were still a little wet from the shower and she struggled not to stand up and lick the water from him. "Um.." She was struggling to put her thoughts together. "I wanted to talk to you."

He walked over to the top dresser drawer and pulled out a pair of black boxer briefs. His back was just as muscular as the rest of him. There was a tattoo over his left shoulder that she hadn't noticed. Before she could stop herself, she stood and walked toward him. Her hand reached out and lightly traced the tattoo. His whole body shivered. He froze but didn't pull away. She traced it again and then leaned in and kissed it. He didn't move. His towel was still around his waist and his boxers in his hands. She wanted to reach around and take the towel off just to get a look at the rest of him. "What does this mean?" She lightly traced the tattoo again.

He turned around so slowly at first she didn't know if he would answer her. His voice was raspy and quiet. "The dates in the middle are my tour dates. The names around the outside are the names of all the buddies that I lost over there."

"It's beautiful." Sophie swallowed hard when she realized her hand was now on his chest. His eyes burned into her and her legs became weak.

"Soph, what are you doing here?" His whisper was barely audible and he covered her hand with his. "I said I needed time."

"I know." Tears formed in the corner of her eyes. His skin was so warm and she wanted to melt into his arms. "I gave you five minutes."

He bent down to her ear. "That isn't what I meant." His breath tickled her ear and her nipples instantly hardened. He took a step closer to her and pulled her chin up to meet his eyes. Her eyes were teary and he couldn't help himself. His mouth brushed her lips so lightly she wasn't sure it was real. He stepped back and waited for her response. She crushed her mouth back into his, her tongue running along his lips asking permission for entry. He opened his mouth and the kiss deepened. His hands tangled into her hair and she ran her hands down his sides and around to his back. A small moan escaped her lips and he smiled. He was a goner.

Mark broke the kiss and took a step back. "Where is Chad?" He asked out of breath.

"I sent him to my room for a few min…"

He threw her on the bed and the kiss became frantic. Flipping onto his back, he pulled her on top of him. The towel came loose but he never broke the kiss. His hands ran up the back of her legs and cupped the most perfect ass he had ever touched. She rocked her body against his erection and he sucked in a gasp of air. She sat up and wiggled to where she wanted to be. The boxers she wore were so loose, his erection slipped into one of the stretched out openings for her legs. He could feel her hot skin and the moisture pooled there just for him. He rubbed himself lightly through her folds and found the hard nub waiting for his touch. She rocked hard and he almost entered her.

"Stop." Mark's hands grabbed her hips and held her in place. Her eyes were glassy with need and her lids heavy over them. She wiggled in protest. "Sophie, Stop. We have to think about this. You know how I am. And I don't think this is you."

She stroked his face. "This is me with you. Something about

you drives me nuts. And you aren't the person you think you are. You are a good man, Mark."

"I don't do relationships. I can't." Mark's heart thundered through his chest. Was that true? He didn't know anymore. She drove him crazy and he didn't want her to leave his sight.

She gave him a small reassuring smile. "If you don't want to do this, I understand. You drive me crazy and I will take whatever I can get from you, even if it's just this trip."

He scrubbed his hand down his face. Was he going to turn her down? If he did this, could he walk away? His brain spun. He wanted her. Hell, he wasn't even in her yet and he was ready to lose it. She was so wet for him and she was so innocent.

He rolled her onto her side. "Give me a minute." He grabbed his phone and sent the text as fast as he could.

```
Can't make breakfast.
Please remove Caleb
and Chad from
Sophie's room and
keep them
busy.  I need one
hour - M
```

Chapter 8

"You are OK with just this? Just Jamaica?" Mark held tight to her hips watching her nod her answer. "And, what about Caleb? He's my friend."

She sighed and nuzzled against his neck. "I know. He's great. But I don't feel the same way he does. Does that make me have to stop going after what I want?" She traced the line of muscle along his shoulder and down his chest. "Just Jamaica. And after that, you have no ties to me if that's what you want."

In one quick move, he had her shirt off and was kissing her from her neck to her stomach. Her nipples grew hard as he gently sucked each one, giving them the attention she was craving. She arched into his touch. He groaned when his hand traveled into her boxer shorts. She was so wet and it was all for him.

"Can I take these off?" Mark's gaze burned into her. She nodded and bit her bottom lip as he slowly removed her shorts. "Oh Sophie, You are so beautiful." He bent down to kiss her. The kiss was slow, breathing her in, memorizing every part of her mouth. She wrapped her arms around his neck, heat shooting to every part of her.

His hand trailed down her belly and stilled. Her whole body trembled. "Are you sure?" His breathing was jagged and his voice was low and sexy.

"Yes." She smiled but her body continued to tremble.

"I'm sorry. I don't know what's happening. I have never felt like this before. I need you to touch me. This is already so much better than anything I have ever felt."

His fingers caressed her folds and one slid slowly into her core. He hissed at how hot and tight she was. He needed to please her first because he didn't know how long he could hold on. His thumb found her hard nub and rubbed it slowly. Her hips bucked and she dug her nails into his arms. He smiled at her and continued his sensual torture. Her eyes were wide and bright and never left his. As he slid a second finger in, she moaned. His pace increased as her eyes began to close. His thumb rubbed harder over the bundle of nerves begging to be touched. She threw her head back and yelled his name, eyes shut, room spinning, as her release overtook her. Her body clamped down around his fingers and he growled. He had to have her now.

He reached into the drawer to grab his wallet. He prayed he still had a condom in it. Sighing in relief, he pulled out the foil packet and ripped it open. Her eyes were wide and satisfied and she pulled him on top of her. "I'll go slow. I promise. And if you want me to stop, I will."

"No," Sophie was out of breath. "That was amazing. I don't want gentle. I want all of you."

He entered her in one slow stroke. She was so tight he had to stop and take a breath. She wrapped her legs around him to allow him to sink deeper and met him stroke for stroke. Her body was so responsive to his every move. As he picked up his pace, he kissed her mouth, then her breasts and she fell apart again, more moisture pooling around him and he couldn't hold back any longer. With one final stroke, he threw his head back as his own release shot through him with more force than anything he had ever felt.

He collapsed against her on the bed, his breathing erratic and took her mouth in a kiss more frantic than when they had started. "Holy hell Sophie." He gasped. "You are amazing." He pulled out of her, his body instantly regretting the separation. He tugged her into his arms and nuzzled her neck.

Her whole body shook as she hugged him back. His eyes met hers with a look of panic. "I'm ok." She smiled. "I have just never.. It's never.." Her eyes dropped to his dog tags.

He put his head into his hand, leaning up off the bed to get a better look at her. His smile widened at how shy he had become. "You are so responsive to my touch."

She smiled and met his eyes. "It's never been like that." A deep blush crept up her neck to her cheeks. "Can we do it again?"

Mark laughed and leaned down to kiss her. "We can if I have another condom in my bag."

"If you don't, you better text your boy Ryan because you aren't leaving this room until we do that again."

Her sudden self confidence made Mark jump off the bed and fish through his bag. When he found what he was looking for, he held it up to her. Her grin widened and she held her arms open to him. "Come back to bed."

****

"There's the man of the hour." Rich yelled and waved to Mark as he entered the restaurant. There was an unspoken secret between them that Rich would never betray.

"What took you so long? I thought you were just

showering?" Caleb glared at him.

Mark smiled. "My real estate agent called. She found a couple places she wants to show me and it took longer than I thought. She's faxing them over now."

"Are we losing you already?" Rich winked as he finished his last bite of breakfast. "Molly will be sad when she hears you are already moving on."

Mark just laughed as he signaled for the waitress. "Well, she found me two places in Beverly Hills and one in the Hollywood hills so it's not a done deal yet. I have to like something first." He took a sip of his juice and noticed Caleb still glaring his way. "What?"

"Have you seen Soph?" Caleb's whole body was tense.

"I did," Chad got up from the table. "She was leaving your room about an hour ago. I'm heading back up to brush my teeth. You want me to find her?"

"Speak of the Devil," Rich waved as Sophie and Molly rounded the corner. They were both wearing bikinis and carrying towels.

"Mark, these were at the front desk for you. Do you need to tell me something?" Molly shoved a bunch of papers in front of his face. "Are you leaving us? You stayed with us all of two nights." Molly pouted and took a seat on Rich's lap.

Mark grabbed the papers Molly had thrown and looked at the faxes as he ate some pineapple. "No offense Molls, but when you and Rich get back from the honeymoon, I don't want to be aware of anything you two may be doing." He looked up at Sophie and patted the chair next to him. "Hi."

She blushed. "Hi." She took a seat next to him and smiled at the rest of the group. She was sure she imagined the stare she got from Caleb. No need to be nervous now. She wouldn't keep it from him if he asked. But she would not intentionally bring it up. Her eyes scanned over Mark's body and up to the papers he was so carefully examining. "What is that?"

His eyes met hers. He pulled her chair a little closer and

handed her the top sheet. "This, my dear, is a house that I am looking at next week." He studied the second sheet and her gaze dropped to the paper. She gasped when she saw the 2.4 million dollar price tag. Reaching under the table, his free hand found her knee and she settled. "You like it? Or this one maybe?"

Why he was asking her, he had no idea. Two times in the heat of passion did not a relationship make. Relationship? He froze. Did he want that? She took the second page from him and looked it over. He felt her body completely relax under his touch. He liked touching her.

He jumped when Ryan's hands came crashing down onto his shoulders. "Package delivered bro. Now let's go and check out the nude beach."

"I'll be right behind you. I have a couple calls to make." Mark handed Sophie the third sheet and smiled at her. "What do you think?"

"Um, I don't know." Sophie cleared her throat. "It's hard to tell from the pictures. They look nice." She offered Mark a sexy smile and he took the hint.

"They have a business center here, right? Come on, let's go look at the virtual tours. I need a woman's opinion." Mark grabbed her hand and pulled her a little too quickly from the group. "We'll be back."

When they hit the stairwell, he slammed Sophie against the wall and lifted her off the ground. She wrapped her legs around his waist and kissed him hard. He cocked one eye brow and looked at her "Again?"

"Again." She held him tight as he carried her up the stairs.

****

She was completely satisfied. She had never been touched like that. She had never been kissed like that. And her body had certainly never responded like that. All those stories from her friends about how great sex was and she finally understood. Mark was nothing like Shawn. Heat poured from Mark's fingers, his eyes were hungry, and his skill was unmatched. She knew she was in trouble. They only had one more day in Jamaica and she would have to let him go. The instant connection she felt with him scared her.

"I lost you for a minute," Mark rubbed his hands down her arms and pulled her closer. "You ok?"

She traced her finger over his dog tags and down onto his muscular chest. "I am better than OK. I was just thinking about how crazy it will be when we get home."

"A lot will happen. Molly is going to be married." He took a deep breath. "I haven't seen my parents in a few years. And I have got to find a house. Hell, my office isn't even unpacked yet." Her trailed kissed down her neck and into the crook of her collar bone. "Tell me more about you. I want to know everything." The words were out of his mouth before he knew what he was saying. Did he want to know everything? His head spun.

"Well, I have a sister, Layla. She lives in Atlanta. She practically raised me. My dad left when I was little and my mom didn't handle it well. We moved around a lot until she had enough heartbreak and started drinking. Layla was in high school by then so she took over being the parent. We haven't had any contact with her since I graduated from high school." She rolled onto her back and stared at the ceiling. "I went to a small college in Georgia and met Shawn. You pretty much know the rest. I love my job. I love LA. And I have a huge fear of becoming the crazy cat lady."

Mark's laugh was deep and he kissed her on the mouth. "There is absolutely no way you are becoming the cat lady. Don't ever let what the prick did to you doubt yourself. You are gorgeous and you are smart and my guess is you'll never even own one cat."

She laughed, "Well, that's good because I don't think they allow cats in my building."

****

Mark spent the better part of the afternoon talking with his Realtor and trying to get Sophie out of his mind. He knew this needed to remain a secret so nothing would tarnish Sophie's reputation. And they still had one day. His phone buzzed and he looked down at the screen.

"Can't reach my back. Where are you? Getting burnt."

Mark smiled as he sent a message back. "Not your back I want to reach."

A minute later she responded. "Mr. Moretti, Are you getting fresh?"

His smile grew. "Meet me in the ocean in ten minutes and find out."

Bing. "The waters warm. Come find me."

Mark grabbed his key and headed down the hall. He was almost in a jog when Rich yelled from down the hall. "Marco, we are heading out to parasail. You down?"

He stopped and turned to see Rich, Ryan and Caleb looking at him. "I would love to boys. But I have something I need to do. I will catch you after." As he turned around and picked up his stride, he swore he heard Ryan say something rude but he didn't care. He had somewhere he needed to be.

Stepping out onto the beach, he noticed the dark clouds rolling in. It had rained for a half hour every day here. People were beginning to pack up and head inside. He noticed a beautiful blond about waist deep in the water and couldn't help himself. He kicked off his shoes, threw down his towel and sprinted into the water. The splashing caught her attention and a big smile appeared on her face.

Without even looking around, he grabbed her into his arms and kissed her passionately as the rain began to fall. She wrapped her legs around him and he walked her deeper into the ocean. She rocked against his erection and he moaned. "What are you doing to me Sophie? I can't get enough of you."

She smiled as the rain fell hard around them. "Should be go in?"

Mark laughed. "Hell no. This is exactly how I like you. Hot and wet."

****

"What's with the shit eating grin?" Caleb smiled at Mark as he took the stool next to him at the swim up bar.

"I've been looking for you guys. Guess parasailing was out, huh?" Mark ordered a Red Stripe and winked at Rich.

"Now you with the shit eating grin. What am I missing?" Ryan shoved Rich off his chair. "What's up Marco? You finally get some?"

Rich came sputtering out of the water. "Can I not just be happy my boy is back? When the rain clears, we're going to try to go up. Guy says he can take us up whenever."

"Sounds great. Sign me up. I'm yours for the night."

"No more house hunting?" Caleb gave him a questioning look that had Mark feel his first wave of panic.

"Nope. I'm leaving that for when I get home. Have someone in mind to help me look." Mark tipped his beer to the bartender and was served another one.

"Let me guess." Ryan laughed. "You already have a chick back in LA. Three nights home and my dog's still got it."

"Actually, no. This girl's on the east coast." Mark ignored the looks the men were giving him.

Rich choked on his beer. "I'm sorry. What?"

"Don't read too much into this. It's just someone who is going to have a much better opinion on houses than I would." Mark faced them all as they stared.

"Ok if I bring a date to the wedding?"

Chapter 9

Mark jogged down to meet Ryan at the nude beach. "Two days in a row? There has to be more to do than lie here checking out the competition. It's our last day. Let's go do something else."

Ryan settled on his elbows. "No competition baby. You're late. You've been missing the show." He pointed a thumb over to where Molly and the rest of the bridesmaids were sunbathing topless.

"Holy hell, don't ever make me look at my sister if she isn't wearing a top." Mark buried his head into the towel. He grabbed his phone and shot off a quick message. "I see you."

Bing. "I see you too. You're wearing too much." Eye contact and sizzle, Mark licked his lips.

Sophie squirmed on her towel as the butterflies took flight in her stomach. This was their last day in Jamaica and her heart hurt. After their tryst in the ocean yesterday, she knew she was gone. The power that this man held over her heart in such a short time was incredible. And he had said she was doing something to him too. She couldn't dare dream this could last longer than this trip. He had been very honest with her about what he wasn't looking for. She returned Caleb's wave and lay back down.

Caleb came back out of the water and took a seat next to Ryan. "He notice Molly yet?"

He laughed and took a long swig of his beer.

"We need to leave here. I cannot have you guys staring at my sister." Mark got to his knees and Ryan laughed.

"We aren't looking at your sister. Dude, that chick was made to have me inside her." Ryan lifted his sunglasses.

"Stop," Caleb shut him down. "Don't talk about her like that. Seriously, that is totally disrespectful. And haven't you learned anything from your time out with her?"

"This is different. We're in paradise, she's almost naked. Look around you. This place is sex." Ryan shifted his swim trunks.

"The place may be different but the girl's the same. And let it go already. She's got feelings for someone else." Caleb shot a glance at Mark.

Feelings? Mark wanted to throw his fist in the air and yell but he had promised to keep it quiet. And if Caleb was talking about someone else, he would look like a fool. Where was the hard ass bachelor he worked so hard to personify? Gone. He was in major trouble.

"Look at her Man. She's hot." Ryan whistled and all the girls looked. He waved and they ignored him. "Right now may be the only chance you get. Drink it in. You may never see this again."

Mark's fists clenched at his side. He saw red. Never had

he been so affected by someone. Was it fear? Was he scared he was going to lose her? The answer in his brain was a resounding YES! Seven days was all he had known her. Certainly not long enough to feel anything. But now he knew she had feelings for someone and he couldn't help but think it was him.

His desire to punch Ryan in the jaw was overwhelming. He tried to tune his voice out and he took deep breaths as he settled back onto his towel. Grabbing his phone he typed as quickly as he could, "I hear you have feelings for someone. Care to elaborate?" His hands shook as he watched her look at her phone. She blushed.

"If you don't go talk to her, I will." Ryan shoved Caleb to

get his attention. "This is Hedonism. You are supposed to be balls deep in someone here."

"Really?" Caleb shoved him back. "She's been pretty clear how she feels about me. And she's my friend so please, stop. You take shit way too far."

Ryan stood up, slipped on his Red Sox cap on and smiled. "You snooze you lose brother."

Mark became hyperaware of Ryan's every move. He watched him like a hawk as he walked toward the girls and took a seat in between Amber and Sophie. Amber shoved him in the back and Sophie just started laughing and covered her face. He couldn't hear what he was saying but knew it wasn't going well for him. The moment he reached a hand out and rubbed it down Sophie's leg, Mark was on his feet.

His sudden movement got Caleb's attention. "I'm sorry man. I'm really sorry."

"Just go," He waved Mark away.

Mark's footsteps pounded in the sand as he approached the group. Ryan's hand was still on Sophie's leg and he was furious. Sophie had not made any move to brush him off and was still topless and covering her eyes. This was not happening on his watch. He marched right into the middle of the group and slapped Ryan's hand off her leg, "Excuse me brother." Ryan jumped back and Mark plastered his body on top of hers. His kiss was hard and demanding and she smiled against his lips.

Everyone's jaws dropped and Molly stifled a surprised squeal. Ryan sat there stunned. The world disappeared around them as she wrapped her arms around his neck. "Wondered how long it would take you." Sophie laughed against his lips and Mark knew he was falling in love.

****

Everyone gathered at the beach the last night on the Island. The breeze was strong and slightly chilled. Drinks were flowing freely and the conversation was easy. Music blared in the background and the sounds of wild parties surrounded them. Sophie huddled closer to Mark and smiled. "You smell nice." She nuzzled her face into his neck.

"So, wait a minute. Wait a minute." Molly giggled as she slid into Rich's lap. "How long has this been going on?"

Sophie blushed, "A few days."

"A little longer for me." Mark shocked the whole group, including Sophie. "What? I'm not a heartless bastard." He wadded his napkin up and threw it at a stunned Ryan.

Molly gasped. "By chance is that what was wrong with you on the plane?"

Mark laughed. "A little bit, yeah."

"You had me totally freaked out. Why didn't you tell me?" Molly jumped up and hugged him tightly. "Why did you hide this from me?"

"Wait, what happened on the plane?" Sophie gazed up at Mark with her big chocolate eyes. "You were sitting right by us."

"No, he got up and had a temper tantrum freak out in the back of the plane scared the stewardess enough that she was forcing liquor down his throat to get him to calm down."

"Molly, really?" Mark gave her the death stare. "And that folks, is the brother sister bond at its finest."

The group laughed but Sophie's gaze remained on Mark the

whole time. "Where was I? Why didn't I know this was going on?"

Caleb cleared his throat. "You were with me. You had fallen asleep across my lap." All eyes turned to Caleb and for a moment, there was silence. "Ok, Ok, let's not make a big deal out of this. Moving on. I want to propose a toast to our wonderful hosts for bringing us to the hottest place on earth, thereby reminding us that are single that we are lacking…"

"Speak for yourself Allen." Ryan laughed and raised his glass. "And for giving us a chance to see the entire bridal party naked, so we know what to picture under those dresses. And for loving us enough to be a part of the day that you both say I do."

"And for loving me enough to welcome me into your group with open arms." Sophie raised her glass. "And to Amber for forcing me take off my top and be subjected to more of Ryan's bullshit."

"Speaking of taking your top off. To Chad, for graciously offering to sleep in Caleb's room tonight." Mark winked at Chad and raised his glass.

"Oh, I did? OK. And to Mark for finally coming home to all of us after all those years of finding yourself and making a fortune. We are glad you decided to grace us with your presence again." Chad raised his glass.

"Here Here," Rich toasted his friends. "To all of you guys for being an honorary part of the Dickerman family for all these years. You've given me more brothers and sisters than I ever wanted. And thank you for allowing my mother to dictate the next three weeks of your lives. You knew what you were getting into and you still said yes. And finally, to my wife to be; you said yes, even though I was the older creepy kid on the playground lusting after his best friend's sister. I love you baby."

Molly wiped a tear from her face. "No. To all of you, because I thought my life was full when it was just me and Markie, but now I am inheriting the whole adopted and dysfunctional Dickerman gang and I couldn't be happier."

Mark got to his feet. "Sappy time is over. We have to meet down here at 9 AM to catch our flight. And I am ready to head upstairs." He held his hand out to Sophie and she took it and smiled. Her heart broke knowing this could be their last night together.

****

As soon as the door slammed shut, he was on her; his hands slipping under her shirt and hers grabbing at his buttons. If this was to be their last night together, Sophie was going to give him something to remember. The kiss was passionate and she moaned into his mouth. His answering growl was all it took.

Sophie dropped to her knees, unzipped his pants and pulled

his shorts and boxers down in one tug. He was gorgeous and she wanted to remember every inch of him. His head fell back as she took him in her hand. She circled her tongue around the tip of his erection and slowly eased his large length into her mouth. The heat of her mouth was like molten lava. His hands tangled in her hair. "Sophie," he moaned. She continued her slow, agonizing torture and Mark was weak at the knees. "I need to be inside you. Now." He yanked her up from the ground and threw her onto the bed. Landing on top of her with a bounce, she giggled. "The things you do to me woman!"

He trailed kisses from behind her ear, down her collar bone and stopped. He hung his head. "What's wrong?" Sophie reached down and pulled his face up to hers.

He kissed the tip of her nose and sighed. "We used the last condom this afternoon." He rolled off her frustrated and was shocked when she followed him. She straddled his perfectly chiseled hips and smiled. She slid her hand down his erection and centered it under her core. "What are you doing?" His firm grip held her in place.

"I'm making love to you on our last night in paradise. I've been on the pill for three years and I have only been with one person. When I found out he had been unfaithful, I was tested. I'm clean." She smiled at him.

Mark sighed. "I have never been unsafe with anyone. And testing is part of my yearly physical. I'm safe."

"Then I trust you." She slid down him slowly, watching his face relax and his eyes close. "Look at me."

He hissed in a breath as the sensation of skin on skin hit him. Nothing had ever felt hotter and she was so tight. Taking his entire length in, she rocked slowly on his hips, his hands guiding her and meeting her stroke for stroke. He smiled when his eyes met hers and her strokes became more urgent. She panted and grabbed at his chest. His hands travelled to her breasts and he caressed her nipples. She moaned.

"I love the way we fit together." He smiled with his eyes shut as she rode him toward the release they both desperately craved.

****

Caleb dragged his suitcase down to the front desk and took a deep breath of the ocean air. The time in Jamaica had been fun and although he hurt over the loss of the girl he craved, he was glad that his best friend seemed happy and that maybe he had become a different person since the last time he had been home. He knew finding Ryan a steady woman was going to be a challenge but a little calm in his life would be nice. The sound of Mark's quiet voice dragged him from his thoughts.

"No, I know this sounds crazy. And I hate to call and wake you up so early. I am heading back to LA today."

Caleb glanced around the corner and saw Mark on his cell phone whispering. His back was to Caleb and he instantly felt like he was hearing something he shouldn't. He prayed he was wrong.

"I just need you to come out to LA." He paused. "I understand you think that and I don't care. I will fly you out here; I'll rent you a car. Hell, I will buy you a damn car. I just need you."

Caleb noticed Ryan heading his way and shook his head and pointed. Ryan joined Caleb against the wall with a confused look on his face.

"I will fly you out first class. I need your help finding a house. I can't pick something alone." Mark huffed like a child. "Listen, it's a week out of your life. It is house hunting and a wedding and you can meet my family. I wouldn't ask you if it didn't mean everything to me. I will pick a bachelor pad, you know I will. If you are going to be staying there, don't you think you need to help me pick something that might be appealing to a woman? I will narrow it down to two or three and then you can help pick it."

"What the hell man?" Ryan whispered to Caleb. "What are we listening to? Who is that?"

"I don't know but he isn't talking to Sophie and I will be damned if I let her get hurt."

Caleb shot back a little louder than expected.

Mark laughed. "Thank you. I love you, I love you, I love you. I will have my secretary call to make the arrangements. I promise you won't regret your time with me." He snapped his phone shut and walked away.

"Shit." Ryan shook his head and put his hand on Caleb's shoulder. "I'm out of this. It's your girl. I've got your back either way. But no secrets. I mean it."

"Hi guys." They both jumped as Sophie headed toward them from the shuttle bus. "Have either of you seen Mark?"

Caleb swallowed hard and shook his head no.

Chapter 10

The ride to the airport was quiet. Sophie glanced over at Mark asleep in the seat next to her and her heart broke. She couldn't believe their time together was coming to an end. She stared at his tussled hair and reached out to smooth it down in front. His soft moan made her smile. She would miss him. She knew it would kill her to see him around town but a promise was a promise and she intended to keep her word. Their affair had been a vacation only deal. She would keep up her end in hopes if they ever had the chance to do it again, he would know she could handle it. But in the early morning light of their last few hours, she wasn't sure how she was going to let him go.

"That feels nice." His voice was groggy and a slow smile reached his eyes.

Noticing she was still running her hands through his hair, Sophie smiled. "I'm sorry. I didn't mean to wake you."

"I like when you touch me." He put his head down on her shoulder and shut his eyes once more. His hand reached out to hold hers and he sighed. "I probably like it too much."

"Don't say that. We had a deal and if I'm supposed to keep it, you can't say things like that." Sophie looked out the window as a tear slipped down her cheek. His sigh told her everything and she knew the wall around her heart he had broken down was going to take a while to rebuild. She never thought she would feel something for anyone again. Mark had proven her wrong. As he snuggled in closer to her, she laid her head on his. She didn't believe in love at first sight. Heck, she hardly believed in love anymore. But Mark had changed that and it was time to say goodbye. Three hours on the cramped shuttle did little to help her anxiety. She would never find anyone else like him.

The airport was chaos. Everyone hurried to get bags checked and boarding passes printed and despite his best efforts to change his seat with Caleb, Mark was frustrated when they told him it couldn't be changed. He doubted Caleb was going to give up his seat freely so he resigned himself to sitting across the aisle again.

Boarding the plane, he shoved his computer in the overhead compartment. What she said on the shuttle had been his worst fear. She did only want a fling. He wanted to respect her wishes but somehow knew he would work hard to change her mind. If Sophie truly meant vacation only, he would spend the entire flight holding her hand. Technically it was still vacation until they landed in LA. He winked as she sat down and she gave him a sad smile.

"What's with the frown baby?" He took her hand. "You OK?"

"Just kind of sad to see vacation coming to an end I guess." Sophie buckled her seat belt and took a deep breath. "No freaking out on this flight, deal?"

Mark laughed. "Tell pretty boy over there to keep his hands off you and we have a deal." Caleb shot him the bird and looked out the window. "Come on C. Lighten up brother."

Caleb stood up and grabbed his bag. "Just get your shit and switch with me. I am not going to be able to handle your mouth the whole way home."

With a huge grin, Mark took Caleb's seat and pulled Sophie into him. He trailed kisses down her jaw and onto her neck. Her body tensed and he smiled. "Technically it's still vacation so I have a little more time with you."

The hours flew by like minutes holding Sophie in his arms. He had never wanted to be so close to someone. She had been asleep for the last hour and he watched her in awe. Her thick lashes covered the most beautiful brown eyes he had ever seen. Her skin was warm and tanned and her soft hair smelled of Jasmine. Her legs were perfection, long and lean and he longed to spend just one more night with her. Even asleep, her responsiveness to his lightest touch was something he would never forget. As the lights of LA appeared in the distance, a strange tightening took hold in his chest. He gently shook her awake. "Sophie, we are almost home."

Her sleepy eyes met his and he leaned down to kiss her. The kiss was gentle and loving, not frantic like all the others. He cupped her face and he swallowed her moan. Her hands travelled around his neck and her fingers tangled into his hair. There was no hurry despite the ticking of the clock. He pulled her even closer and sighed as the plane touched down.

"Can I give you ride home?" It was worth a try.

She smiled and leaned against him. "I have my car here but thank you for the offer."

"Well, let me walk you to your car." He grabbed his bag and threw it over his shoulder so he could carry her suitcase. When they arrived at her Ford Escape, he put her things in the back seat and buckled her in. "Soph, I had the most amazing vacation. Thank you for that." He kissed her cheek and squeezed her hand. Her faint smile broke his heart. He shut her car door and watched as she pulled out of the parking garage.

Grabbing his phone, he sent her a message. "I miss you already."

****

Sophie glanced at her phone and saw the text. She rubbed her chest. It felt like her heart had been ripped out. Handing the money to the attendant at the parking garage, she felt the first tear hit her cheek. .

She tucked her phone into her purse. There was no way she could respond to him. Four years with Shawn and a terrible break up and she never felt this pain. The first sob broke loose as she hit the highway. She couldn't wait to hide under her covers for the rest of the weekend.

****

"Good morning Mary." Mark walked to his secretary's desk and stopped with a few notes. "I have an appointment to meet my realtor at four today. Does that fit into my schedule?"

"Your last meeting is at 2:00, Mr. Moretti, so you should have plenty of time. The movers also moved your things into the corporate suite while you were gone. Can I get you some coffee?" Mary's face lit up when he smiled at her.

"Please call me Mark. Mr. Moretti is my father. And I can get my own coffee. You won't have to do that." His laugh made Mary blush. "I have just a few things for you. If you could send flowers to this address, I would appreciate it. Lots of flowers. An obscene amount of flowers." He handed her his American Express and the address of Phantom House Publishing. "I also need you to make copies of my schedule for the next two weeks and put them on my desk. But most importantly, please make travel arrangements for her. I need first class out here the week of Molly's wedding. She can stay with me but she may want a car. Her name and number are here and she's expecting your call. Whatever she wants, she gets. Keep this credit card with you."

"I will get right on that Sir." Mary began to type in the

address of a florist on her computer.

"No. Sir is worse. Mark is good." He grabbed his briefcase and strolled into his nearly empty office. Looking out the window, he couldn't help but wonder what Sophie was doing. He didn't know her routine. He didn't know what time she got up in the morning or what she wore to work. He sighed. He had kept his word and not made contact over the weekend. But today, he couldn't shake the feeling of dread not waking up next to her. His chest felt empty. He would send flowers and wait. The next move had to be hers.

His morning finance meeting dragged on longer than expected. When he got back to his office, he found his schedules and a copy of the travel itinerary. Mary was good. He was lucky to have her. His last secretary had been too nervous around him and he found himself doing things himself instead of asking her. The phone vibrated in his pocket and he reached for it. "They are beautiful. There isn't enough room in my cubicle for all of them. Thank you."

He smiled at his phone. Progress. "They aren't nearly as beautiful as you are."

Bing. "Flirt."

His grin widened. "What are you wearing?"

Bing. "Is that seriously the best you've got?"

Mark chuckled. "I've got some others."

Bing. "Try me."

"You know what would look great on you? Me."

Bing. "Does that really ever work?"

Laughing, he clicked on the camera icon and took a picture of himself and sent it. "You'd be surprised."

Bing. "I've missed your face."

Clicking on the attachment, his breath hitched. The return picture was of her gorgeous tanned leg wearing black stilettos. "Have dinner with me. Tonight." He typed back quickly.

Bing. "Ok."

"I have a meeting at 4:00. Dinner at 8:00?"

Bing. "My place. Bring take out. And Mark, wear that tie."

"Wear those shoes." Mark groaned as he put his phone back into his pocket. Maybe it wasn't over after all.

****

Four houses later, Mark was pulling into Sophie's apartment complex with a front seat full of Chinese take out. He grabbed his duffle bag and suit out of the back of his car and balanced the box of Chinese in his other hand. Presumptuous he would be spending the night? Yes. Would he leave even if she asked him to?

Probably not. No. God he hoped she was still in those shoes. His blood was boiling by the time he got to her front door. He knocked and held his breath.

Sophie answered the door, still dressed in her black skirt and white blouse. His eyes ran down the length of her body, stopped at the shoes and growled. She laughed. "What's with the bag and the clothes?"

He tossed his things across the couch and put the Chinese food on the table. "No talking," he growled as he shoved her up against the wall. Grabbing her hair, he tilted her head back and kissed behind her ear. She shivered. He kissed and sucked at her neck, wanting to mark her so everyone knew she was his. He loosened his grip on her hair and grabbed the hem of her shirt. In one pull, her shirt was off and he was devouring her breasts. Her whimper was all the encouragement he needed. He picked her up and she wrapped her legs around his waist. His mouth met hers in a kiss that left them both panting. He yanked the skirt up to her waist. "God I missed you."

"I missed you too." She was breathless as she reached down to undo his belt. Her hands shook and he smiled against her mouth.

In one tug, he ripped her panties off. "I'll buy you new ones." His fingers plunged into her core and she bucked against his hand. "Always so ready for me." His thumb found her hard bundle of nerves and she threw her head back and moaned.

Her teeth grazed along the muscles in his neck and down to his shoulders. He had the most perfect hands. He knew exactly where to touch and what to do. Her breathing became more frantic and his fingers picked up speed. "Please Mark," she begged.

"What do you want baby?" His eyes met hers and she came undone. She bit his shoulder as her orgasm took hold of her whole body. Her body clamped down on his fingers and she cried out as wave after wave hit her. He continued at the same speed and smiled as she gasped. "You are so beautiful."

She clawed at his pants. "Need you. Now." Her voice cracked

as she tried to unzip his fly. "Mark," she gasped. "I need you." His zipper finally gave way and she grabbed his erection. His hands continued their erotic torture. As her second orgasm began to build, she didn't think she could take it. "Oh God."

"Just let go." He knew every inch of her. He knew the curves of her face and the roll of her eyes as pleasure built in her body. He listened to her breathing and when it became frantic, he shoved into her in one long stroke. She cried his name as her pleasure hit her so hard she had to dig her nails into his back to keep from going boneless in his arms. His strokes were fast, hard and frantic. His lips met hers in the most passionate kiss she had ever felt. His pleasure shot all the way down his spine and he yelled her name as he erupted into her.

Sweating and out of breath, he set her down on the floor and kissed her forehead. She closed her eyes and leaned into him. He placed a soft kiss on each eye lid then down her cheek to her mouth. She smiled against him. He reached up and cupped her face and pulled back. "Hi." He whispered.

"Hi." She smiled.

Chapter 11

Mark startled awake and looked at the clock. 4:00 AM. He was covered in sweat. It had been the same dream for three nights in a row. Sophie was leaving him and he couldn't stop her. He looked over at her and sighed. Her light breathing indicated she was still asleep. Tonight they would need to stay at his place. They had spent the past three nights together, sleeping in short bursts and spending the rest of the night with their bodies entwined. But every morning, the same panic hit him. There was so much left unspoken and he knew he would need to tell her how he felt. Would she run? That would kill him.

He reached over and brushed her hair off her forehead. She

moaned and his body instantly responded. He pushed the covers off them and climbed on top of her. The kisses were slow and she opened her eyes and smiled at him. She noticed the look of panic on his face and opened her mouth to say something but Mark stopped her. "Shhhh. I need to do this. You are so beautiful. I am so lucky."

He kissed her deeply and passionately. His tongue claimed her mouth and her body came alive. His hands remained on her face and the kiss continued as he entered her. He swallowed her moan and slowly pumped into her body. He pushed up onto his arms and looked at her. His green eyes locked on hers as his body continued it's slow pace. Several times, he leaned down to kiss her, never picking up speed, never putting more than a few inches between them. "God Soph, I don't know what's happening to me."

His eyes met hers again and she came apart. He pinned her with his body and claimed her mouth as pleasure rocked through her. She whimpered as he kept his strokes slow and steady. She grabbed for his hips, begging to pick up the pace but he captured her hands and held them above her head. "Not today baby. I want to make this last." His heart leaped and for the first time in his life, he felt safe and loved. The realization hit him like a lightening bolt. He loved her. As his flight instinct kicked into full gear, he bit down on her shoulder. He wouldn't run. He knew the risks but loving her was no longer an option. Her eyes were closed and her breathing was clipped. "Open your eyes. Look at me. I need you to see what you do to me."

Her hands grabbed the sheets and held on while the most powerful orgasm of her life hit her. His eyes burned into her. His face so intense, she could feel everything he was feeling. The pleasure kept going and she bucked off the mattress. She screamed his name as her climax continued. The pleasure so intense it was almost painful. His mouth crashed down on her lips as her walls continued to spasm around him.

Just as his orgasm hit, he leaned back and looked at her once more. Her eyes were wide and wild and he couldn't hang on any longer. As the last tremor of his body subsided, he sighed. "You've wrecked me Sophie."

"You've wrecked me too, Mark." She rubbed gentle circles on his back as he leaned in and hugged her. She smiled. This was a risk but she was going to take it. "I've been wrecked since the first night on the beach when we sat and talked."

His eyes went wide and he looked up. "Really?" He laughed. "I was a goner when you hit me with that damn cart. I really think you had me then." She giggled and he sat up. "Come shower with me. I need you near me."

****

Mark paced his office. His head was all over the place. It was impossible that he had fallen in love with her so quickly. He didn't fall in love. The only women he had ever loved were his mother and Molly. He had promised himself he would never let this happen. He slumped into his chair and put his face into his hands.

"Markie?" Molly's voice was quiet but it still made him jump. "Are you ok?"

Mark looked up at his sister and smiled. Her face always lit up the room and he was so proud of her. She was everything to him. "Hey kiddo. What are you doing here?" He wrapped his arms around her and hugged her tightly.

"I was downtown and thought I would come say hi. I brought you some of your favorite cookies. I haven't been sleeping much so why not bake?" She smiled and put the container on his desk. "I think I am so excited and nervous about the wedding I just can't think about anything else."

He immediately dug one of the fresh white chocolate chip cookies from the container and sighed. "This is why I love you so much. No one bakes for me. Rich is a lucky man."

"I miss you. I didn't realize you would be moving out so quickly. And to come home from Jamaica to find your things gone was a little bit of a surprise."

"Molls, it was just easier to be downtown as I get settled in. And I want you and Rich to have your space right before the big day. I know Mrs. Dickerman must be driving you nuts and to tell you the truth, it was a little easier to dodge her living on my own." He took another bite of his cookie and laughed. "I want you to be happy and I didn't want you worrying about me all the time. I didn't think I should announce it while we were on vacation. You flipped when you saw the fax from the realtor."

"So how is the house hunting?" Molly stole a cookie and leaned back in her chair.

"Well, I have found a few I like. Most of them in the Hollywood Hills. My favorite is on Hercules Drive but if I am going to drop 2.5 million dollars, do I want my address to be Hercules Drive? I have narrowed it down to three and I will decide next week. I have a friend coming in to help. It needs to be perfect because I want to lay down some roots."

Molly's jaw dropped. "Seriously? Are you really going to stay in LA?"

Mark sighed and leaned closer to her. "I have a few things to stay for."

"Like?"

"Well, you and Rich. And I assume you will be having my nieces and nephews so I will need to be around for that." Mark winked and whispered. "And Sophie."

"You like her. You really like her." Molly teased him but stopped when his face became serious.

"I think I more than like her. I know, it's crazy. Everything I do right now has her in mind. I'm driving myself crazy. My poor secretary must think I am losing my mind."

Molly's eyes were locked on his. She studied his face, like it was the first time she was ever really seeing him. Her slow smile reached her eyes and her face lit up. "Mark, there is no one in the world I love more than you. It's not crazy. Sophie is fantastic. The first time I met her, I loved her. She's so real and normal. Don't get me wrong, I love our friends. But she is so.. hmmm. Nice."

Mark threw a piece of his cookie at her. "I don't do nice. I don't do strings and feelings. I do easy and unattached. It's not normal. By nature, men are not supposed to be monogamous. I think I'm having a heart attack. Stop laughing. I'm serious. I feel sick to my stomach all the time. I can hardly eat and I certainly can't concentrate. Stop laughing." Molly had tears running down her face. She snorted and covered her mouth. "Molls, I'm serious. This is a crisis of epic proportion. What if I screw up? What if I screw her up? What if I lose her? Why are you still laughing? Shit Molly."

"You aren't going to screw it up. Don't be such a pansy. She's perfect for you. And she is obviously bright because she is falling for you too. Although, she is meeting Ryan for lunch today. You may have some competition."

Mark's face went blank. "Ryan? Why?"

Molly shook her head. "Stop worrying. They are talking about his birthday party. Caleb was supposed to go too but his book deadline is next week and there's no way he can get away from the office."

"Thanks, Molls. That makes me feel so much better. I think I would have liked it better if Caleb were going. Ryan is a player."

Laughter from the doorway drew their attention away from the conservation. "Did Mark Moretti just call someone a player?" Rich's laughter was contagious and Molly followed suit. "I was worried since you were taking so long. I didn't realize Mark was telling jokes. Let me have a seat. Tell me another one."

"Nice to see you too Bro."

"No seriously. I heard you calling Ryan a player and I wondered if maybe you had amnesia or something terrible like that." Rich kicked his feet up onto the desk.

"You guys think you are really funny don't you." He pressed the buzzer on his desk. "Mary, can you make me an appointment with Neil Lane for

Monday?" Staring at his shocked friends, Mark laughed. "Who's laughing now?"

Molly covered her mouth and a tear slipped down her cheek. "Are you serious? Are you doing what I think you are doing?"

Mark sat back in his chair and crossed his arms. "Is it a bad idea? Am I crazy?"

"Marco, what are you doing?" Rich sat up straight. "I was joking. Don't do anything drastic just to be a jackass."

"I don't think it's drastic. I think it's romantic." Molly jumped from her chair and landed on his lap. "This is the best news. Are you seriously going to ask her? Oh my God, mom is going to have a heart attack."

"Molls, you can't tell anyone. You need to promise me. You too Dickerman. If I am really going to do this, I am only going to do it once. It needs to be in my own time. Got it?"

Rich stood up and shook his hand. "I am shocked man. But your secret is safe with us. Now don't screw it up."

As Molly and Rich headed for the door, Mary entered his office. "You have an appointment with Mr. Lane at 3:00 on Monday. I have already cleared your schedule."

"Thank you Mary. Now if you will show my guests to the elevator I can get some work done." Mark laughed as Rich flipped him the bird. Was he crazy for doing this? Possibly. Could he imagine even one day without Sophie? Absolutely not.

Chapter 12

"Thanks for picking me up." Sophie climbed into the front seat of Caleb's car. "Mark is going to try to get by but if he doesn't, will you be my hero and take me home?"

Caleb laughed. "I'm surprised Mr. Perfect is letting me pick you up. Considering it's Ryan's birthday and he knows Ryan so well, I am sure he will show up. He's not going to let him get anywhere near you."

Sophie punched Caleb in the arm and settled in. "Very funny. Ryan is harmless."

Caleb raised one eyebrow at her. She was so lucky that he still wanted to remain a big part of her life despite the crash and burn in Jamaica. "Keep telling yourself that." His laugh made her smile.

They rode in silence the rest of the way. Caleb breathed her in. Her perfume awakened every part of him. He knew she would never be his. But in that single moment in time, it felt right to be with her. They pulled into a parking spot. He looked over at her and leaned his head back on the headrest. "You look good, Soph. I guess whatever this is with Mark agrees with you."

Ryan yelled for them as they entered the nightclub. There were several tables reserved and as Caleb went to get their drinks, Sophie had a seat. She fished through her purse in search of her phone to send Mark a message.

"Well, don't you look good enough to eat." The familiar voice made her drop her phone.

"Holy shit. What are you doing here?" Sophie shifted in the booth and looked Shawn right in the eyes.

"Work thing," He took a sip of his beer and reached out to touch her hand. "I'm serious Sophie. You look great."

Caleb cleared his throat and Sophie's panicked look hit him like a ton of bricks. He set her drink down in front of her and faced Shawn. "Caleb Allen. And you are?"

Shawn shook his hand but his eyes didn't leave Sophie's. "Shawn."

The name made him cringe. Sophie had been a wreck for months after she had found him in bed with his secretary. Here he was, in the flesh, touching her like he still owned her. Caleb sat down next to Sophie and put his arm around her. "Well, Shawn, I wouldn't mind if you took your hand off my girlfriend." He pulled Sophie closer and kissed her forehead.

She let out the breath she was holding and moved her hand to Caleb's leg. She smiled up at him, her eyes sparkling with thanks. "Don't get jealous honey. There's nothing left there."

Ryan walked over smiling. "Is it finally swap night?" He laughed and pointed to Caleb.

Sophie's eyes pleaded with him and he swallowed hard. "Ryan, this is Shawn. Shawn, Ryan." Sophie kissed Caleb's neck and snuggled in.

Understanding dawned on Ryan's face and he sat down. "Dude, I don't know how you let such a hot piece of ass get away. I've been trying to get her to leave Caleb and give me a shot but she won't." Long chug of beer and wink. "Anyway, Marco just came in and I thought I would stop by and say hello. I guess I will leave you to it."

Caleb turned and watched Ryan meet Mark at the door. His eyes were on them and if looks could kill, Caleb would be saying his goodbyes. Ryan held his arm and pointed. Mark's face shifted to Shawn and his jaw clenched as Shawn stared at Sophie. Ryan shook his arm to get his attention and started talking more frantically. Mark laughed and walked toward the table.

Caleb's body stiffened and Shawn looked up at Mark. "How's my favorite couple?" Mark laughed as he plopped down next to Shawn. As he loosened his tie, his eyes roamed Sophie and looked back at Caleb. "Caleb." He nodded.

Sophie fidgeted in the seat. "Mark, this is Shawn. My ex." Her voice was higher than normal and she cleared her throat.

"Well, this must suck for you." Mark smiled at Shawn. Shawn was wedged between him and the wall. He wasn't getting up any time soon. "She looks great, doesn't she?" Shawn cleared his throat and took a long chug of beer. "You should have seen her last week. Topless in Jamaica and having the time of her life. Those tan legs wrapped all around this guy here. It was a sight to see."

Shawn looked at Sophie. "There is no way you went topless." His voice was almost a growl.

She smiled. "I did. Guess I just needed the right people around me so I could really find myself." She snuggled so close to Caleb that he blushed.

"They couldn't keep their hands off each other. Constant sex and it hasn't stopped yet." Mark didn't take his eyes off Sophie.

"And it's incredible," Sophie smiled at Mark.

Shawn finished his beer and moved to get up. "I'll get it man, stay." Mark waved the waitress over. "It is incredible. She might even be in love with him. What do you think Caleb?"

Caleb's face was bright red and he shifted uncomfortably in his seat. Shawn looked at Mark with his brows raised. "And you would know this how?"

"Get up Allen," Mark stood and waited for Caleb to move. When he did, Mark sat down and gave her a deep kiss and Sophie melted into his arms. Caleb laughed as Shawn's jaw dropped. "You are the most beautiful woman in the world,

Soph. I can't get enough of you."

"I do love you," Sophie shook as his hand ran down her back.

"I love you too, Soph." Mark brushed the hair out of her face. "Let's go home." As Mark stood up and took Sophie's hand, he noticed his line of friends staring at him. He smiled at the shock on everyone's face. He looked at Shawn. "Thank you for being a douche bag. I honestly don't know where I would be without her." Sophie laughed and hurried out the front door with Mark.

****

As Mark put his Audi in park outside his building, he looked at Sophie. She had been quiet the whole ride. He cleared his throat and she jumped. "Everything ok there champ?"

She smiled at him. "Sorry about the Caleb thing. I panicked."

Mark laughed. "It's fine. At least it was Caleb. Shawn's a jackass. If he would have touched you again, I would have beat his ass."

Sophie laughed. "Were you there the whole time?"

He smiled a tight smile. "I walked in when he sat down but Caleb beat me to the table. Seeing him touch you wasn't much better. I do appreciate how protective he is over you though."

She walked into the elevator behind him and Mark pushed the penthouse button. She looked up at him and he laughed. "It's our corporate suite. It's not mine. I have narrowed the house search down though."

She shifted uncomfortably. "Thanks for what you said at the club." She played with her earring and wouldn't meet his gaze. "It was nice to see Shawn a little shocked."

Mark stared at her. "Look at me." Sophie blushed and met his gaze. "I meant what I said."

"Mark, don't.." Sophie took a step back. The pulse at her neck went crazy.

He grabbed her hand and put it on his chest. "Do you feel this?

You do this to me. No one else ever has." He lowered her hand to his pants. "And you do this to me. You, Sophie. No one else."

She gasped as he pushed her back against the wall of the elevator. He bit her bottom lip and tugged it. His hand ran up her thigh and pushed her panties aside. His fingers plunged into her core, instantly slick with wetness. He licked his lips. "And this, this is all mine."

His fingers continued to pump in and out of her as the elevator door opened to the penthouse suite. He kicked his foot out to hold the door open and continued his fast pace. She clung to his shoulders and shook. He ran his thumb through the wetness and swiped it across the hard nub that made him so happy. "You are all mine, Sophie. No one else is to touch you." He squeezed her nipple through her shirt and her pleasure dropped her to her knees. Mark pulled her up. "Now that we are clear, get in here and let me make love to you."

****

Mark flipped the eggs in the frying pan and looked over at the bacon on the skillet. Sophie had spent the night with him and despite a change in scenery, the same dream had jolted him awake. He had dressed quickly in a pair of sweatpants and gone for a run to clear his head. Sophie was still asleep when he arrived back home so he showered and dressed for the day. He had told her he loved her and spent half the night showing her. His nerves were shot. Tomorrow he would be picking out a ring, and possibly putting an offer on a house. He prayed she felt the same way he did.

"The coffee smells delicious." Sophie yawned and leaned in to hug him. He smelled of mint and man and she grasped a handful of his black t-shirt. Her eyes met his and he smiled a half smile. "Why are you up so early? It's Sunday. Come back to bed."

Mark wrapped his arms around her, her body melting into his. She rubbed her hands up the back of his shirt, memorizing each muscle. His strong shoulders met his perfect back and she touched him freely. Pulling back, she rubbed her hands down his chest, to his sculpted abs and her favorite V that dipped into his loose fitting jeans. He was perfection. She leaned in to kiss his chest and sighed. "I love you Mark. Please don't pull away from me. I know you have been having nightmares. Please talk to me."

Mark pulled her tighter. "I'm afraid to lose you. I've never felt like this before."

Sophie smiled at him, her eyes glistening with unshed tears. "You aren't going to lose me. I'm afraid too. But I would rather be afraid and have you than lose you because of fear."

Mark scooped some eggs onto her plate and poured some juice in a glass. "Sit down. I need to talk to you. I have a crazy week coming up. Work is going to be really busy and I am not sure how much time I am going to have. I just want to know that you won't run from me. The wedding is in less than a week and I need to know you are with me."

Sophie smiled. "I am with you. I know your job can get crazy. I will be here for whatever time you have. But if you are disappearing for a week, I'm going to need a little reminder of what I am waiting for." She walked to him and took his baseball cap off.

Mark smiled and lifted her onto the kitchen counter. She wrapped her legs around him and he growled low in his throat. "You are the most beautiful woman in the whole world. And I am so lucky because I am the one that gets to touch you." He pulled her t-shirt off and sucked in a breath when he realized she wasn't wearing anything else. Gently, he kissed her collar bone, up her neck and behind her right ear.

"No, you have it wrong. I'm the lucky one. You are gorgeous. Such a hunk." She laughed. "You are way out of my league."

"Don't say that. You are the most amazing person in the world." His eyes flashed with anger. "I never expected to feel anything like this for anyone. And I can't believe I found you. Don't ever say that again."

He tangled his hands into her hair and tugged her head back. His mouth attacked hers, making her gasp. His hips ground against her and she moaned. Digging her nails into his t-shirt, she begged. "Please Mark."

"What do you want baby?" He brushed his fingers across her nipple and tugged the pink puckered flesh.

"You. Now. Please don't wait." Sophie grabbed his shirt and yanked it over his head and made quick work of the button on his jeans. Pushing his pants and boxers down in one fluid movement, she wrapped her hand around his erection and grit his teeth.

"Baby, this is going to be quick." He entered her and began pumping into her recklessly. His eyes were glassy and almost feral.

She felt the familiar tightening in her belly and dug her heels into his back. She threw her head back as her release hit her. Her body clenched and shuttered. She bit his shoulder and he pumped even harder. "I'm never going to be able to let you go."

She held him tightly. "I don't want to go anywhere."

Chapter 13

Mark paced his kitchen. Her flight was delayed and he was getting anxious. The appointment with Neil Lane was today and he smiled. She would know exactly what Sophie would like. He wanted this to be perfect. The knock on the door brought him out of his daze. Show time.

"Layla?" Mark locked eyes with the woman at his door. She was taller than Sophie but had the same big chocolate eyes and pouty lips. Her hair was dark brown and fell to her mid back with shiny curls. She wore skinny jeans, a halter top and red lipstick and had a tattoo on her right arm.

She pushed past him into his suite. "You have got to be

kidding me. You are Mark? Way to go Soph." She laughed and wrapped him into a tight hug. "You are hot. Wow."

Mark laughed. She wasn't shy or timid like his Sophie. She kept him in a tight hug when he tried to pull away. His laugh grew louder when she kissed him on the cheek.

"I'm not sure I want to let you go. I haven't hugged a beefy man in awhile." Layla Barringer stood in his suite, looking around and shaking her head. "My sister hit the jackpot with you buddy. Get my bags and show me around already."

Mark's smile grew bigger. "You got it. Please make yourself at home. Help yourself to anything. The bathroom is on the right and your room is right next door. I'll bring your bag in and we need to get going. We have an appointment."

"Yes sir. Please don't let me sit down after that long flight. That would be too kind." She teased back over her shoulder and walked down the hall to find her room. "I still think it's crazy you needed me here. But now that I see you are eye candy, I think I will stay the week."

"You are too kind." He tossed her a helmet and jingled his keys. "Let's roll Kid."

"What are we rolling in exactly?" Layla looked at the helmet and smiled. "You have a bike? You don't look like a bike guy, pretty boy."

"Don't let these good looks fool you. I happen to have a Ducati that just arrived yesterday from my place on the East Coast and I am drying to ride it. Get your ass in gear, let's go."

Mark led Layla down to the garage. He strapped his helmet on and straddled the bike. Layla squealed. "Oh my God. I have to drive this. Can I drive? Please pretty boy. This is amazing. I have a bike but it is nothing like this."

Mark couldn't help but laugh at her. She was nothing like Sophie. She jumped up and down begging to drive. "I'll tell you what. I will drive us there, you help me with this and I will let you drive it. Now stop jumping and get on."

She wrapped her arms around him and they sped out of the parking garage. She leaned into the turns with him and loosened her grip on his waist. He was worried he would never get Sophie on his bike. Layla was a natural. It was a short drive to the appointment and she huffed her disappointment when they stopped.

Her eyes widened at she took off her helmet and noticed the name on the store. "Why are we here?"

Mark climbed off his bike and smiled down at her. "Layla, I need to ask you a question." She shifted uncomfortably. "I love your sister. I never thought I would love anyone but she's amazing. Sophie means everything to me. And you mean everything to her. I know she really only has you. I want to ask your permission to marry your sister."

Layla launched herself off the bike and wrapped her arms around his neck. "Yes. Yes. I am so excited for her. She deserves this so much. She needs some good in her life. Does she know?"

Mark shook his head and took her hand as they walked into Neil Lane's store. "She has no idea."

****

"Ryan, come here man." Caleb slowed the treadmill from his run and yelled over the crowd to Ryan. He had been doing a training session but Caleb didn't care. This was important.

"Dude, do you not see that babe I am training?"

"I don't care. Does Moretti have a bike?" Caleb pointed out the front window of the gym at the Ducati sitting in front of the jewelry store. "I swear to God I just saw him with some brunette. She was hugging him and then they walked in there holding hands."

Ryan looked out the window stunned. "No way man. It couldn't have been. Besides, what would he be doing over there? And not with Sophie?"

The men stood in the window staring at the bike for a few minutes. When they didn't come right back out, Ryan went back to his training session and Caleb picked up his pace on the treadmill. He would run five more miles and call it a day. He had taken a half day from work to spend some time with Ryan at his gym. He had been promising to come by for months and he needed to blow off some steam.

Movement across the street caught his attention. "Um, Ryan?"

Ryan moved to the window and his jaw dropped. Mark was coming out of the store, holding hands with the most beautiful woman he had ever seen. His heart raced and he shook his head. "Who is that?"

Caleb reached for his cell phone. "I have no idea man."

Ryan grabbed his hand. "Leave it alone Allen. Or at least ask

Mark about it before you go blowing this out of proportion. You owe it to him to ask. And you owe it to Soph." He looked back out the window and his eyes locked with hers. His breath caught in his throat. She smiled at him and he froze. Her gaze returned to Mark and she hugged him, holding tightly to a little jewelry bag. "What the hell just happened?"

****

Layla was star struck. She had just met Neil Lane and helped pick out the most gorgeous engagement ring she had ever seen. Sophie was a lucky girl. Mark was gorgeous, adventurous and very rich. She held his hand and dragged him to the bike. "I can't believe I get to drive this. Thank you." She jumped up and down and then jumped into his arms. "You are the best brother in law in the world." She looked across the street and noticed two men in the gym staring at them. She smiled at them before Mark cleared his throat.

"Are you sure you want to drive this?" He dangled the key in front of her and pulled it back when she grabbed for it.

He fastened her chin strap and grabbed the bag with the ring. When she was seated, he eased in behind her and put his hands on hers on the handle bars. "Layla, I am going to let you drive, but first, I am going to hold on for dear life."

Layla elbowed him and started the bike. "Oh pretty boy, if you weren't taken…" Her sentence died as they launched into traffic.

****

Caleb arrived at the office late the next morning and slammed his office door. He had tried to call Mark the night before and left a voice mail that had yet to be returned. He ran his hand through his hair and put his head on his desk. His brain was at war with his heart and his heart was winning. He still loved Sophie and more than anything, he wanted to be with her. But at what cost? His head told him that there must be a logical explanation for what he had seen. But as she entered his office with a timid smile, his heart leaped and overpowered his thoughts.

"Caleb? You ok?" She was so beautiful. Her soft yellow dress showed off her tan and her blond hair was pulled into a loose pony tail, showing off her long neck.

He shivered. "I will be. I need to ask you something."

"Ok." She sat down in the chair opposite him and smiled.

"Did you talk to Mark last night?" Caleb shifted papers on his desk, not making eye contact.

"No. He has a really busy week at work. He told me we wouldn't talk too much this week. Why?"

Caleb flinched. "Soph." His voice was quiet.

She sat up straighter. "Why Caleb? What's happening?"

Clearing his throat, he leaned across the desk and took her hand. "I saw him yesterday. He was with some woman. Ryan says it's probably nothing. And it probably is. But it didn't look like nothing to me. And I tried to call him last night to ask him about it but he never returned my call."

Sophie's face was blank. Her eyes remained locked on his. "What did it look like Caleb?"

He hung his head. He should have ignored his heart. He felt like the worst friend in the world. "I don't know. They seemed pretty friendly. God, I shouldn't have said anything. I feel like shit. I'm sorry Soph.

It's probably nothing. I'm going to call him again."

Caleb hit the speaker button on his phone and called Mark's office. "Mr. Moretti's office. This is Mary. May I help you?"

"Hey Mary, Caleb Allen. Is Mark in?" Sweat broke out across his forehead.

"I'm sorry Mr. Allen. Mr. Moretti is off this week. Can I give him a message for you?"

Caleb froze as Sophie's face fell. He had broken her heart. He was an asshole. "No thank you Mary. I will try his cell phone." He hung up and took Sophie's hand again. "Shit, Soph. I'm sorry. I'm still jealous and I am sure my mind is making things up. Maybe you should try his cell?"

A tear rolled down her face and she whispered. "I can't. What if he's cheating on me? Oh God."

"Then he would be a fool. Want me to try his cell?"

As Sophie nodded her head, Caleb hit the speaker button again and dialed the number he knew so well. Was he setting their relationship up to fail so he would win Sophie? He wasn't sure. He prayed he wasn't but as the phone began to ring, dread settled into his bones. He was hurting her and assuming the worst about his best friend.

"Moretti," Mark was out of breath when he answered,

shushing someone or something in the background.

"Yo, Marko, it's Caleb. What's up man?" Caleb winked at Sophie. Maybe this wasn't bad news.

"Not much C. What's up with you?" His hand covered his phone and his words were to muffled to make up.

"Hey, I was just wondering what you were up to today."

"I'm working. Listen, I've got to run. Work is crazy. Can we catch up later this week?" Mark laughed and asked the driver if she knew how to drive a stick and to stop messing up his car. "I really have to call you back."

The phone went dead and Caleb's eyes froze on Sophie. The blood drained out of her face. Her hands shook and more tears formed in her eyes. He stood and wrapped her into a hug. "I'm sorry Sophie. Go home. Take the day. Call him. Maybe he is with a client. Maybe this is nothing. Please call him. I feel terrible."

Sophie hugged him hard. "Did it look like a client Caleb?"

"No Sophie. It really didn't. I'm so sorry."

****

"Have you ever driven a stick? You are killing my car." Mark laughed at Layla as they tried to make their way up the long driveway of a house his realtor had told him would be perfect.

"Listen, I really have to call you back." Mark ended the call and frowned at Layla. She just laughed as she stalled the car again. "You were better on the bike."

"Get over it pretty boy. You could buy a bunch of these. Why do you have this car anyway? An Audi? I would have expected to be picked up in a limo or something. Don't get me wrong, this car is awesome and I would drive it in a second but.. Sorry, I am babbling again. I know you aren't used to constant talking."

Mark smiled and thought of Sophie. "Soph is pretty quiet." He sighed.

"Oh gag. You've got it bad. When did you know you loved

her? When do I get to see her? When are you asking her?"

"Slow down Dr. Phil." Mark laughed and waved at his realtor, Beth. "You can see her Friday at the rehearsal. And I am thinking of asking her at the wedding. May get Molly and Rich involved in the proposal. I thought maybe even during the reception since Molls has asked me to sing. We will talk about it tomorrow night when they come to dinner. Come on kid. Let's see if this is the house."

Mark looked over the gray stone exterior of the house situated at the top of Beachwood Canyon. He sighed at the three car garage. "This one is how much?"

The realtor shifted her papers. "2.2 million but we can offer less. It was built in 1991. 5,500 square feet of living space and the lot is about 15,700 square feet. Give it a chance Mark. This has a rooftop pool and a sauna. And you would be tucked away from city noise here. You can see the Hollywood sign from the roof."

"Million?" Layla cleared her throat.

Mark patted her back. "Come on. You check the closets for me kid."

She smacked him and ran ahead into the house. She gasped. "Mark, get in here. You have to see this kitchen. It's huge. And white."

Mark walked through the four bedroom, five bathroom house. The closet space was the size of an additional room and knowing he would be spoiling Sophie, he knew that would be a plus. The pool and Jacuzzi were separated by a wall in the pool and he liked the flow of the water back and forth. The view was breathtaking, the ocean on one side and the Hollywood sign on the other. It would be perfect for entertaining but something felt off. "The bedrooms are pretty small Beth. I am willing to pay more if we can get some more space. I want to have kids and I want to be able to see the pool without having them sneak up onto the roof. I'm sorry. It's just not it."

Layla frowned. "You saw the master bath didn't you? The huge tub? The huge mirror?"

"Ok, on to the next. You want to see the short sale again? The six bedroom?"

"Yes. I think Layla needs to see that one."

They followed Beth to the house on Deep Dell. He had narrowed his favorites to three and he wanted Layla to see them. It was a short drive to the Mediterranean house that he thought could be home. "I really want your opinion on this. It's bigger than the last. It was built in 2005 so it doesn't need as much work. In fact, I could move right into this one."

Layla wandered through each of the six bedrooms. All of

them had an in suite bathroom. The four car garage made more sense to her since she had already seen two cars and a bike and that wasn't including whatever Sophie was driving these days. The first floor was almost all stone. Was it marble? The large winding staircase made her gasp. She sat down on the floor of the theater room and shook her head. Everything was open and the view was gorgeous. The pool came off the living room and was surrounded by a large deck that overlooked LA. Tucked away on the third floor was one bedroom, with a private balcony and bathroom. She smiled.

She joined Mark in the kitchen, where he was sitting on the counter looking over some mortgage forms. "How much is this? And can he afford it?"

Beth smiled at her. "Yes he can. It's a short sale. It's been on the market for 100 days. They are asking 2.4 million. Payments will be approximately $9,000 a month depending on how much he wants to put down."

"Hey pretty boy," Layla laughed as he bit his lip looking at his paperwork. "I think we can stop looking. She will love this."

Mark looked up and smiled. "Yeah?"

"On one condition. That little room on the third floor?"

"Yes?" Mark jumped off the counter and put his arm around her to lead her out.

"Well, if I wanted to move here, could I stay in that room?"

"I would love it if you stayed in that room." He hugged her close and looked at Beth. "Ok. Let's make an offer."

Chapter 14

Layla stood at the coffee pot willing the drips to come faster. The trip had provided little relaxation with Mark's obsessive jam packed schedule. Tonight, they would have company for dinner. But today, she planned on making Mark take her shopping and then spending half the day basking in the late afternoon sun. A light rasp on the door drew her from her caffeine meditation. She checked the clock. 6:30 AM.

Shuffling to the door in her pajama pants and fitted tank top, she looked out the peephole and smiled. Adonis number two was at the door.

"Can I help you?" Layla smiled as she met his eyes.

Caleb ran his eyes down the beautiful woman at the door. He didn't even try to hide his appreciation of her scant clothing. He pushed past her into the living room and crossed his arms. "Where is Moretti?"

"Well, come in." Layla huffed and mimicked his stance. "Do you realize how early it is?"

"Well, it's too early for Mark to have company, that's for sure. Did you spend the night? Where the hell is he?"

Layla took a step forward and ran her finger down his tie and moaned. "Aren't you a regular Prince Charming? Before you start demanding answers, I have a question of my own. Who the hell are you?" She licked her lips.

Caleb almost swallowed his tongue. She was beautiful with her sleepy eyes and her bare face. Her dark hair was tied into a loose knot on the top of her head. He stuttered. "I'm Caleb. I am looking for Mark. Do you or do you not know where he is?"

With a big sigh, Layla walked toward the hallway and yelled. "Pretty Boy. Get up. You have company. Some really charming and not at all intrusive guy named Caleb." She waited at the end of hall. "Wow. Even without much sleep, you are pretty. Want some coffee?"

Caleb heard Mark mumble before he walked into the living

room. His hair was unruly and he wore nothing but a pair of jeans with the top button undone. Caleb fisted his hands and tried to calm his breathing. He couldn't believe his own eyes.

"What's up C? Everything ok?" Mark's face fell and he stopped in his tracks.

Clearing his throat, Caleb took a step forward. "I came to ask you a question but it's been answered so I am done here." Turning to leave, Mark grabbed his arm and Caleb tensed.

"Caleb. Why are you here? Did something happen?" Mark's voice grew louder and drew Layla from the kitchen. Caleb turned slowly, meeting Mark's eyes. Anger and aggression flared. Was that hated? Mark's thoughts stopped abruptly.

Well.
Shit.

The punch was square in the jaw and right on target. Mark's eyes filled with stars as he stumbled backward and onto his ass. His world went dark, then just as fast, blurred back into focus. He rubbed his jaw and stared at Caleb.

"What the hell?" Layla ran into the living room to kneel by Mark. She shot Caleb the death stare. "You need to get the hell out of here."

"With pleasure." Caleb slammed the door shut and walked into the waiting elevator.

Mark stood and headed to the kitchen for some ice. He was silent. After grabbing his ice pack, he spit a mouth full of blood into the sink and rinsed his mouth. The bruise was already starting and his head throbbed. He glanced at Layla who stood shocked in the doorway.

"What the hell was that?" Her arms were crossed over her chest and her eyebrows drawn in a straight line. "I'm so sorry I let him in here. Who is he?"

"That, Layla, is my best friend." Mark spit another mouthful of blood into the kitchen sink.

"Well, holy crap. If that's your best friend, I guess I need to wear of a suit of armor tonight to meet your sister."

"Welcome to LA." Mark walked back into his bedroom and shut the door.

****

Where was she? Mark had been texting Sophie all day with no response. His three voicemails had gone unanswered and now he was starting to worry. The incident this morning weighed heavily on his mind but he refused to contact him. He was finished with Caleb's emotional warfare. Whatever was going on, Caleb was on his own to figure it out.

Today had been a wasted day. His head pounded. He had tried to take Layla shopping on Rodeo drive but after just three stores, he was forced to give up. He had bought her a silver charm bracelet and a purple gown to wear to the wedding. Buttering up the sister was priority number one. But today, it took the backburner to the war raging in his skull.

The bruise on his face spread the entire right side of his jaw. What a beautiful souvenir from his best friend. The wedding was in three days and the pictures would be a reminder forever. He sighed as he grabbed his towel and headed up to meet Layla at the rooftop pool. Molly and Rich would be here shortly for a last minute cookout before their lives spun out of control.

Layla was swimming laps, her bikini leaving very little to the imagination. Mark smiled at the knowledge that he could look at a beautiful woman and feel nothing. His heart swelled with pride at the thought of Sophie being his wife. "Looking good LB."

She splashed him as he started the grill and he laughed. "Do you know your initials are MMMMM? Very appropriate." Mark belly laughed as Layla blushed.

"Markie!" A sweet little squeal drew both their heads in the direction of the stairs. She stopped cold when she saw Layla in the pool. "Who's this?"

Layla climbed out of the pool and smiled. Rich's eyes followed her every move and there was no hiding the appreciation on his face. "Hi

Molly. I'm Layla. Barringer. Sophie's sister."

Molly's jaw dropped and Mark laughed. "It's OK Molls. You can say hi. She won't bite."

"Oh my gosh. It is so nice to meet you!" Molly pulled Layla in for a hug. "Does Sophie know you are here?"

"Down boy." Mark slapped his hand onto Rich's back. "Stick that tongue back in your mouth. That's my future sister in law you're ogling."

Molly just shook her head. "I'm sorry you have to be surrounded by cavemen but welcome to my hell."

"I am here to surprise my sister. But it has been nice to hang with Mr. Eye Candy for a couple days. It is really nice to meet you girl I have heard so much about you from Sophie and I was hoping I would get to meet you. I didn't expect all the house hunting and secret shopping. But I am glad I am here."

"Me too. Now come on and tell me about the ring." Molly took Layla's hand and led her to the lounge chairs. "And the house. I can't believe my brother bought a house in LA."

Mark continued to cook the steaks. The salad and vegetables were done and he sang along to the radio while he waited. Steve's career was finally taking off as the new DJ of the hottest radio station in LA. He was so proud of all his friends. Well, everyone but

Caleb. He shook his head and concentrated on the music.

Rich broke into his thoughts. "So, you are seriously oblivious to perfection. How is this possible? Self proclaimed eternal bachelor Mark Moretti being tamed by a shy, timid blonde? I wouldn't have believed it in a million years." Mark turned to face him and Rich gasped. "What the hell happened to your face?"

"I had a small run in…"

"With a douchebag's fist." Layla finished his sentence and Mark cringed. "What? He was a douche. Acting like he owned the place, pushing by me in the doorway. Demanding I get you. Ridiculous."

The song on the radio came to an end and Steve's voice rang out onto the airwaves. "This next song goes out to Sophie. Caleb says he knows you are a closet Bieber fan and this song says it all."

Justin Bieber's 'Fall' came on the radio and Mark froze.

'Well let me tell you a story, about a girl and a boy
He fell in love with his best friend, when she's around he feels nothing but joy...
But did you know that I love you, or were you not aware?
You're the smile on my face and I ain't going nowhere.'

"What the hell is going on?" Mark dropped into a lounge chair next to Molly. His head fell into his hands and his shoulders slumped. Molly reached out and traced his jaw and he flinched. "What the hell is this?" He waved his hands toward the radio. He grabbed his phone and shot Sophie another text.

'What is going on? I need you to talk to me.'

Molly sighed. "I don't know. Sophie wasn't in today. Apparently, she and Caleb had a meeting yesterday. I really don't know what was said but she was crying when she left and Caleb sat in his office in silence the rest of the day. I talked to her this morning but all I could get out of her was that she wasn't feeling well and she needed a few days. Said she would see me at the rehearsal."

"Caleb as in the Caleb that hit you?" Layla sat up straighter. "That wasn't Sophie's boss Caleb was it?"

"Caleb did that to you?" Molly's eyes watered. "Why?"

"I have no idea. He showed up here and woke me up this morning. Didn't say much. Just punched me in the jaw and slammed the door. I have tried to reach Sophie all day. She won't talk to me." Mark glanced at Layla as her phone rang. Her face said it all. She stood up and walked to the stairs before answering. "Molls, I wanted to ask her to marry me at the wedding. That's what this dinner was about. I know you wanted me to sing something else at the reception. But I wanted to sing Marry me by Train and ask her at your reception. I know that might have been stealing some of your thunder but I wanted to share the day with all you guys." Mark rubbed his face and sighed. "What?"

Molly just stared as a tear rolled down her cheek. Her eyes were wide and her jaw dropped open. "Seriously? The reception is perfect but why are you saying it like you aren't going to ask her now?"

"She won't talk to me Molly. Caleb shows up and punches me in the face, now this dedication to her on the radio. Is there something going on? I am blind? Was this not mutual?"

"Mark. Stop." Rich put his hand on his forearm. "This is nuts. There is some logical explanation for this. Well, except for the punch in the face. That's ludicrous. We will all get to the bottom of this. Maybe she really is sick and the two incidents aren't related."

"Dude, if she were sick, you would think she would want me around." Mark stood up and headed to the top of the stairs to eavesdrop on Layla's conversation.

****

"Sophie, calm down. What's going on?" Mark could only hear Layla's side of the conversation but he felt better just knowing Sophie was OK. "Why would he dedicate a song to you? What does Mark have to say about this Soph?" Her eyes met Mark's and she mouthed "she's ok."

As Mark stepped away from the stairs he heard Layla gasp. "Don't you dare go to the wedding with Caleb." His shoulders slumped.

Chapter 15

Mark stood in the foyer of the church. His hair was spiked and messy. The gray button down shirt he wore showed his broad chest and lean waist. His sleeves were rolled up showing his sculpted forearms and his freshly tattooed chest peeked out the top buttons. Layla smiled as she thought of them sitting in the tattoo studio for hours the day before as Mark tried to decide if he wanted to ink his pristine chest. He had decided on two simple stars while Layla tattooed the same on her foot. She sighed as Mark rung his hands together and then wiped them down the front of his pants. She didn't know how this trip would end but she had enjoyed every minute of getting to know Mark. He had quickly become the brother she had always wanted.

"You look good. Stop fidgeting." Layla smoothed Mark's shirt and put her hand on his shoulder to settle his hands. "I don't know what is happening but I do know that the last five days have been wonderful and my sister is stupid if she can walk away from someone like you. Now let's get in there and win her back."

Mark hugged Layla. "You're the best. And if I lose everything this weekend, I know you will always be my little pain in the ass."

Layla laughed and hugged him back. "Well, get used to me, I am moving into that room upstairs in two weeks. I guess that makes the house yours alone for about twenty four hours."

Mark pulled back. "Are you really moving in?"

Layla laughed. "Yes I am. But I promise I won't be there forever. I know you and Soph will end up getting married and do that baby making thing that a sister should know nothing about. Ever. But until then, you are stuck with me bud"

Mark smiled his perfect smile at her and his green eyes sparkled. She stepped in to hug him once more and her eyes locked on the man behind them. His brown eyes were wide as he smiled at her. She held her breath. This was the same man she had seen earlier in the week through the gym window. He turned and walked away down the hall. She was more than happy to watch his perfect back side as he left.

****

Sophie stood quietly in the back hallway with Caleb and Molly. Her light pink dress hugged her hips and ended just above her knees. Caleb had studied her when she first walked down the hall and she had blushed. She played with her charm bracelet as Molly went over her list of the wedding party pairings. She dreaded seeing Mark again. She knew her heart would break. Caleb had been a true friend this week, informing her of what he saw and later, she found out, going to Mark's apartment, confronting him in front of the other woman and defending her honor.

The truth had destroyed her. When she had caught Shawn cheating, she had vowed to never let someone in again. Mark had shattered the walls around her heart and in such a short time, she had loved him more deeply than she had ever loved Shawn.

Her eyes began to water and Caleb took her hand and squeezed. "You are fine sweetheart. One step at a time."

Ryan stumbled into the back hallway, his feet thudding against the hard wood. "Who the hell is the babe with Marco? I wouldn't mind a piece of that."

"Seriously?" Caleb shoved him. "Sophie is right here. Attempt to have some class West."

Sophie turned to walk away when Molly grabbed her hand. "Caleb, don't you dare start shit here. This is my wedding rehearsal and I will be pissed if you cause another scene."

Caleb huffed. "He damn well deserved it Molly. You have no idea what Mark did to Sophie."

"There is no excuse for acting like a total ass. That huge bruise on his jaw will be in my wedding pictures forever. That was totally uncalled for. Change your attitude or leave." Molly's face flushed red with anger.

"Did you hit him?" Sophie glared at Caleb.

"Hell yes I hit him. He cheated on you Sophie."

"What are you talking about?" Molly was fuming.

"I'm talking about Mark cheating with some brunette that I found at his house at 6:30 in the morning. Not cool Molly. Don't even defend him." Caleb threw his arm around Sophie.

"He brought her here for Sophie you jackass. That is her sister. Mind your own damn business Caleb." Molly stormed off toward the sanctuary to begin the rehearsal.

Sophie's whole body tensed and her head spun. She looked at Caleb and went pale.

****

Mark stood with Rich at the altar waiting for the pastor to direct the rest of the wedding party down the aisle. Chad led the men, followed by Steve, Ryan and finally Caleb. His hands immediately formed a fist and he shut his eyes. He was thankful that there were three grown men between him and Caleb. He would hate to make a scene in the church.

Five days of no contact with Sophie solidified his opinion of their relationship. He took a deep breath as the girls were directed down the aisle. Amber smiled at him as she stepped into the church. He cringed.

Claire, Liz and Jessica beamed with excitement as they took their spots at the altar. A lump formed in his throat as he pictured what his wedding to Sophie would have been like. As she stepped through the door way, his breath caught. Her fitted pink dress showed off her gorgeous figure and her hair hung down her back, curled and soft. Her eyes were wild, noticing Layla for the first time and stumbling. Her eyes did not meet Mark's.

"I'm not sure I can do this." Mark whispered in Rich's ear.

"I promise you it will be over soon. I will buy you a beer in about ten minutes." Rich straightened as Molly stood at the end of the aisle. His face softened. His smile was full of passion.

Mark locked eyes with his sister. She was beautiful. He tried to swallow past the lump in her throat. His eyes filled with tears. Everything they had been through together had led up to this moment. His father led her down the aisle. Mark struggled to feel a connection with his parents but was willing to offer a truce for the wedding. This day meant the world to his sister and despite his heartbreak; he would be the perfect best man and an even better brother. He knew tomorrow would be an emotional day. He looked at Layla and she gave him thumbs up. He winked and thanked God that he had someone in his corner.

****

"I love you so much Molls. I am going to be a mess tomorrow." Mark wrapped his arms around her. "You mean everything to me kid."

"Are you mad Dad is walking me down the aisle?"

"Absolutely not. I wouldn't miss seeing you come down this aisle for anything." Mark let her go as Layla joined them. "Besides, I have to keep an eye on LB here. The Ryan attack will be in full force at some point."

Layla laughed. "I don't know who that is but I can assure you I can handle myself."

"I have no doubt about.." Mark's sentence was cut short as Ryan stopped behind him. "We were just talking about you West. This is Layla Barringer. Layla, Ryan West."

Ryan took Layla's hand and a jolt of electricity ran up his arm. Shaking his head, he smiled. "It's nice to meet you. Who knew Sophie had such a hot sister."

Layla rolled her eyes and groaned. "Who knew Mark had such hot friends. Well, except that asshole in the purple." She pointed at Caleb as he approached the group.

Mark turned his back to Caleb. He would not ruin this day for his sister. He took a few deep breaths as he heard Caleb introduce himself to Layla. Her voice was strained at the introduction. Stepping into Mark, she tossed her hair over her shoulder. "I wish I could say it was a pleasure, but that would be a lie."

Mark grinned at her. "If you have something you would like to talk to me about, I suggest we take this outside. Otherwise, I would appreciate it if you excuse us as we finish our conversation."

"Mark?" Sophie's voice was quiet. She made eye contact with Layla and attempted a nervous smile.

Mark looked her right in the eyes. "Sophie," he nodded.

"This is low. Even for you Moretti." Caleb took a step back.

"Caleb, I am not playing these games with you. I really have no idea what has you wound so tightly, but back off." Mark shoved his hands in his pockets to keep from loosing his cool.

"One Barringer sister isn't enough for you? You have to go out and bag the other one?"

Layla jerked her head around to face Caleb. "Listen jerk. You have no idea what you are talking about. Don't you dare judge me or my relationship with Mark. I have spent five days here and the one thing I know for certain is that he is a good man and you're an asshole."

"LB, I will meet you in the car. I need some air." Mark turned to walk down the aisle.

His mind was dazed. Outside, an afternoon storm was just beginning. The rain fell softly on his face reminding him that he was still alive and life went on. He placed both hands on the hood of the car and leaned in. The rain picked up and fell heavy on the back of his neck and shoulders, feeling like slivers of glass. He shivered as the wind whipped past him. He felt empty.

He looked at the front of the church he had been baptized in. He and Molly had spent countless summers here at camp and more Sunday mornings than he could count. All of the memories included his baby sister. It had been them against the world. As he planned his engagement to Sophie, he had pictured being in this church, waiting patiently for her to become his wife. The idea now seemed so far fetched.

It had only been five days since he and Layla had gone to see Neil Lane about an engagement ring. It had been four days since she had helped him pick out the house that Sophie would like the best. It had only taken Layla one day to realize the kind of person he was now He had gone on with his life, excited at what was to come. All the while, his best friend had been turning the woman he loves against him. Looking back, he could understand why Caleb had felt he has been unfaithful to Sophie. The Mark of the past would have done something as despicable as that. The old Mark was a bachelor looking for his next conquest. That Mark Moretti didn't live here anymore and had become an entirely different person with the help of Sophie. But he thought Sophie had known him better than this. He had every confidence in her and their relationship. It ripped his heart out to know that her opinion of him was so low and that she believed he could be that cold. It was a punch in the gut that his best friend would drag his name in the mud for a chance at the woman he loved so much.

Shaking his head, he got into the driver's side of the Mercedes SUV and waited for Layla to come out. They would be going out somewhere with a lot of drinks.

****

"Caleb, calm down." Rich put his hand on Caleb's chest after the second insult was thrown at Layla. "This has nothing to do with you at all. I think Sophie and Mark should talk and get to the bottom of this. You will not, and I repeat not, ruin tonight or tomorrow for Molly. Am I clear?"

Sophie's tears ran down her face. Caleb put his arm around her waist and pulled her to him. Her stomach churned. "I don't understand. Why are you here Lay?"

"She's here because Moretti couldn't be satisfied with one woman. This is a great opportunity for her. Mark is loaded. He's the perfect guy. I am so sick of hearing that." Caleb slapped Rich's hand off his chest.

"You know what?' Molly stormed down the aisle. "I have had enough. That attitude of yours changes tonight Caleb or don't bother showing up tomorrow."

"I am not going to stand here and be spoken down to. I am an adult and will not tolerate this. Ryan, can you walk me out please?" Ryan nodded and joined Layla as she started to walk toward the door.

"Wait." Sophie yelled and ran after her. "I just want to understand why you are here Lay. What's happening? Is there any truth to what Caleb is saying?"

Taking a calming breath, Layla turned back to her sister. "Of course it isn't true. Not one bit of it. And you if you don't know me, or Mark for that matter, well enough to even think it could be true just proves you don't know us at all."

"Then why come?" Sophie cried.

"Well, he thought you would be happy to see me, but that surprise flopped. He also needed help to pick out the perfect house, where you would be living with him and he wanted to surprise you with that too. I guess that surprise flopped to. But I guess the biggest reason I am here is because we no longer have mom and dad and Mark thought it would be nice to ask someone if it was ok if he asked for your hand in marriage. We picked out a really gorgeous ring. AS A SURPRISE. Also a flop I would say. So if you will excuse me, there is a beer somewhere in my future screaming my name and I am going to find it." Layla didn't turn around on her way out; just left Sophie standing there with her mouth hanging open

Chapter 16

Mark couldn't believe today was the day. His little sister, the love of his life until a few weeks ago, was marrying his best friend. Straightening his tuxedo jacket, he smiled remembering the first time Rich had confessed to loving her. It was a lifetime ago. And despite moves to different colleges, finding careers and building their futures, they had never once waivered in their commitment to each other.

Mark envied them. What they had was rare. He had made a promise to himself years ago that he would not fall in love. Aside from his sister's fairytale, he had been a non believer. Watching so many relationships crumble, he had been certain he would not fall victim to the madness. But then Sophie rammed her cart into his ankles and his world had turned upside down. He had craved her the second their eyes met. The few weeks he had known her had been the best of his life. He had fallen for her completely and in record time. He hadn't stood a chance.

Reality had different plans for him. One cruel twist of fate, mixed with a possessive friend and a plan he thought would be flawless, and his world had crumbled. He didn't regret asking Layla to come to LA and help him. She had been light when his world went dark. But his ignorance in thinking things would go his way had been his undoing.

Never imagining that Caleb would turn on him was mistake number one. Trust your brothers. Leave no soldier behind. You go, we go. It was all engrained into his head. Throughout every tour overseas and the hundreds of men that had fought beside him, he never expected enemy number one would be a best friend. And even now, he refused to justify his actions to a man he had considered family his whole life. The yellowing bruise on his jaw was a stark reminder of the day it all changed.

As the music started, he glanced at Rich. Strong, powerful, loyal to a fault. And now, after all the years of feeling like his brother, he was becoming family. He smiled as Rich took a deep breath. "I'm really happy for you. You deserve this man. Thank you for loving her as much as I do."

Rich smiled, a light sweat covering his forehead. "I just have to keep breathing. Passing out is not an option."

Mark laughed. The world was at peace again. Ryan was still Ryan, chasing a new woman every night. Rich was still Rich, humble and dedicated. Mark was still Mark, bachelor to the end. And Caleb, well, he didn't know Caleb anymore. And that was OK.

Sophie stepped into the sanctuary. Her hair was swept into a knot as the base of her neck, loose curls framing her face. She was everything he had wanted. Everything he still wanted. The walls around his heart were now reinforced and although he would have traded the world for one more night with her, her lack of faith in him was enough to keep him focused on the real reason they were here. Love. Love for two people who had each other's backs. Love that knew no limits. Love that created trust and faith.

The music changed and his sister appeared in the doorway. She took his breath away. He would have fought to the death to protect her and now that right was going to someone else. His eyes watered as she winked at him and walked toward her future. He rubbed his hand across his chest, feeling like his heart would explode. The gesture was not lost on Sophie. He felt her gaze burning into him but he would not look. She had made her choice when she had believed Caleb without a second thought. She had broken him when she arrived with Caleb at the church. He would hold his head high, lose like a gentleman and never, ever fall again.

****

The reception hall was exactly what Sophie had imagined. The hotel ballroom sparkled. She took her seat at the head table, between Rich and Ryan. It had been torture to smile, despite her love for Molly. She had fallen for Mark and without giving him a chance to explain, she had believed the worst. Her fear of commitment had cost her the man she loved. She was her own worst enemy.

His reputation had been known from the start. But the man she heard about and the man she knew were two completely different people. Caleb had dropped the bomb on her and she had run for the hills. She couldn't be mad at him. She had no one to blame but herself. She vowed if she ever had a chance to make it up to Mark, she would take it and spend the rest of her days proving she had faith in him.

She looked at her sister. Layla had been her only family for so many years. She trusted her completely. But the fact she had made a surprise trip to LA and was staying with Mark sat heavily on her heart. He had kept her trip a secret. She had helped Mark pick out a house that she would have made her home. She shivered as Layla's words came back to her from the night before. *"We picked out a really gorgeous ring. As a surprise."* He was going to propose. He loved her so completely that he had broken all his rules, fallen hard and wanted to spend the rest of his life with her. And now, he was standing with her sister, his face grim and wounded and she had been the cause.

"Ladies and Gentleman, I would like to call the best man up for his toast. Mark, if you are ready." The DJ interrupted her thoughts. She watched as Mark smiled at Layla and made his way to the stage.

****

The butterflies in Mark's stomach disappeared as soon as he stepped on stage and looked at his sister. Grabbing the microphone, he cleared his throat and smiled. "Molls, you look beautiful. I cannot begin to tell you how proud I am of you." He picked up a guitar that had been leaning on the DJ's booth and had a seat on the stool in the center of the stage. "A million years ago, when Rich and I were hardly old enough to tie our own shoes, he saw my sister for the first time. And I could tell right away that he loved her. He spent countless hours convincing me he didn't because he thought I wouldn't take it well. And I admit, at first, I didn't. Molly could have cared less, which just added to my satisfaction. But as time went on, I watched them together. Rich forever by her side, and Molly slowly realizing what they had was special. And in all the years I have known Rich, I have never seen him look at anyone else the way he looks at her. I kept waiting for life to catch up with them but as the years went on, I understood that what they had was very rare. I'm not going to lie, I was a little jealous. All those nights hanging out with me and Caleb turned into nights with her. Wherever you saw one, you saw the other. Today I get it. I see that you guys are two separate people that together are stronger and whole. I'm not sure I really believed in love until recently. But if you two have even a quarter of what I felt, I have no doubt that you will spend the rest of your lives making each other happy and living for the other. I love you both very much. I am honored to share the day with you. I wish you both an endless amount of love." He raised his eyes to look at Sophie. "I hope that one day we are all able to feel what you feel and have it returned unconditionally. What you have is rare. Cherish it. Trust one another. Be best friends. But most of all, love each other fiercely everyday."

The crowd clapped as he settled the microphone into the stand. Rich wiped tears from Molly's eyes and kissed her gently. When Molly looked up, she mouthed 'I love you' to Mark. Mark winked.

"Molls asked me if I would sing at the reception. I hesitated because it has been a long time since I have done anything like this. Originally they asked me to sing 'God Gave Me You' by Blake

Shelton. But seriously Molls that song sucks." The crowd laughed and He strummed a few notes. "So two nights ago, Molly and Rich came over for dinner with me and the lovely Layla Barringer and although things have not happened even remotely close to how I expected, I played this song for them and everything just clicked. So Moll and Rich, if you would head to the dance floor, I will now make a fool out of myself. Ladies and gentleman, 'Marry Me' by Train."

Forever can never be long enough for me
To feel like I've had long enough with you
Forget the world now, we won't let them see
But there's one thing left to do

Now that the weight has lifted
Love has surely shifted my way

Marry me
Today and every day
Marry me
If I ever get the nerve to say
"Hello" in this cafe
Say you will
Mm-hmm
Say you will
Mm-hmm

Mark finished the song and smiled at his sister. Tears fell from her eyes as she held onto Rich. He dared a glance at Sophie and his breath hitched. She sat transfixed, her eyes full of tears and her face in agony. He looked away quickly, needing distance to keep his heart from breaking even further.

The next hour passed by in a blur. Mark made his way to all the tables to say hello to the people he hadn't seen since he had left home and his shots of Patron had settled his nerves. Being numb was better than feeling anything. The music slowed and Mark felt a hand on his arm. "Dance with me, pretty boy. Come talk to me."

Mark led Layla to the dance floor and took her into his arms. "Thank you for coming with me Layla. You have been a respite for me the past two days. You will never know how much that has meant to me."

"I hate how this has all gone down. I have faith in you. I think everything will work the way it's supposed to." Layla laid her head on his shoulder and shut her eyes.

Mark's hands trembled as he saw Sophie and Ryan heading to the dance floor. Seeing Caleb with her was difficult but knowing what Ryan would be thinking as he held her sent his temper into overdrive. Closing his eyes, he took a deep breath.

"Hey gorgeous, mind if I steal you away for a minute?" Ryan held his arms out to Layla.

Mark stiffened as she left his arms. Sophie took a hesitant step toward him. "Dance with me?" Her voice shook.

Despite his heart's protest, he wrapped his arms around her. Her body fit against his perfectly and it felt like home. His body instantly responded to her. Her body snug against him, her familiar smell, her soft skin against his hard muscles. He groaned and shut his eyes. "Jesus, Soph. You are killing me. I can't do this." He backed away from her but she caught his arm.

"Mark, I'm so sorry. I know words won't ever mean anything but you are everything to me and I would do anything to take it back." She leaned against him once more. "I understand that forgiving me may be out of the question, but please don't shut me out completely. I have missed you so much."

"It all seems like a terrible idea now. But everything I did this week was for you. I love you Sophie. But I don't ever think I will be enough for you. I would have done anything for you." He wouldn't meet her eyes.

Desperate to make him understand how she felt, she rubbed her body against his. "Please come upstairs with me. Please. Let me show you how much I love you. And then you can walk away if you still want to. Just give me one more chance to be with you. Even if it is goodbye."

His pants became uncomfortably tight. He rubbed his hand down her back and she arched into him, her breasts rubbing against his chest. "I don't think this is a good idea. I have been drinking. A lot. And I have to drive your sister to the airport early tomorrow morning. There are a million reasons we shouldn't." He couldn't believe what he was saying. Where was Mark Moretti and who was this person he had become?

Sophie surveyed the crowd around them. When she was sure no one was looking, she ran her hand down his erection and cupped him in her hand. "I don't care. I know you want me. And I want you too. So, let's go." She bit his bottom lip and pulled. The pain sent him into a dizzying spiral.

"This is just sex Sophie. I can't give you anything else. I can't get hurt." He locked eyes with Layla and she nodded. "Do you understand that we are not together? That this is just us needing a release? Do you understand that I am going to make you come, I'm going to get off and then leave?" There he was. The old Mark had returned.

"Yes," She was breathless. "I want you."

Upstairs, things went from fast to frantic. Mark unzipped Sophie's dress in record time. He growled when he saw the new lingerie underneath. Black silk with a red lace overlay barely covered what he couldn't wait to get his hands on. Black garters and more black silk leading to black heels that made her legs go on for miles.

Pushing the cups of her bra aside, he took a nipple into his mouth and sucked hard. They tightened in his mouth and she moaned. Her body arched into him as moisture pooled between her legs, soaking the new panties she had purchased in case she got just one more time with Mark. He unbuttoned his shirt and threw it onto the dresser. His pants and boxers hit the floor and he shoved her onto the bed.

Yanking her panties down, he buried his face in her center. The urgent strokes of his tongue told her he meant business. He circled her clit while two fingers pumped in and out of her. She arched off the bed. Panting, she grabbed Mark's head and tangled her hands in his unruly hair. Her response was all he needed. He twisted his fingers and applied pressure to that spot she loved so much. Her eyes closed and he stopped. "Open your eyes Sophie. I don't want you to have any doubt who is making you come." Her eyes locked with him for just a moment and then he sucked hard on her sweet spot and her world shattered into a million pieces. She screamed his name as the waves of pleasure overtook her.

He shoved into her and hissed. The walls of her core squeezed him as her body continued to pulse. "Shit, always so wet and hot for me." He didn't take his time. He pounded into her as she clawed at his back. Grabbing her leg, he bent it forward so he could thrust deeper. Her body began to shake and he knew she was close. He withdrew and shoved back into her with force and she shattered. His balls tightened and his spine tingled. He moaned as he exploded and emptied everything he had into her. "Shit," he hissed. "I'm going to miss being inside you. You feel so damn good."

Her face was flushed and gorgeous. She grabbed at his head to bring him down for a kiss but he resisted. Pulling out of her, he made his way to the bathroom to clean himself up. A piece of his heart shattered with each step he took. He dressed quickly and fixed his hair in the mirror. "I'm going to go. I can't miss Molly's reception and if I don't leave now, I am never going to want to. We both know we can't go back. Trust is an important thing, Sophie. Without it, we had nothing."

A tear escaped from her eyes. "I'm so sorry Mark. I never meant to hurt you. I have no excuse for believing Caleb. It's the biggest regret of my life."

He pulled something from his jacket pocket. His face fell. "Tonight was supposed to be so different." His voice cracked and he cleared his throat. He sat on the edge of the bed and she sat up. She touched his arm but he pulled away. "I have to go. But I want you to remember this. And us. I have never been in love before and I will not allow myself to do it again."

The light hit the ring he held in his hand. The beautiful Asscher cut diamond took her breath away. The halo of diamonds around it sparkled and she closed her eyes. He studied it for a long moment in silence. His shoulders slumped forward. "Keep this. I have no reason to hold onto it. It will just be a constant reminder of the woman who didn't love me enough to trust me. Look at it often and remind yourself that there will be people who love you so fiercely that you need to take the gamble on them."

Standing and straightening his jacket, he threw the ring on the bed and walked away.

Chapter 17

Sophie sat in her cubicle feeling like the walls were closing in on her. Tomorrow would be a week since Mark walked away from her in the hotel room. She didn't blame him at all. She had destroyed their relationship in one morning when she had chosen Caleb over him. Her chest hurt and breathing was the hardest thing in the world. She had been attempting to edit the same book all week and was making very little progress. She put her head onto her desk, shut her eyes and took a deep breath.

Molly was on her honeymoon so she didn't have her best friend and her only connection to Mark. Layla was pretty quiet. A handful of text messages had done little to reassure her that it wasn't her against the world. Caleb had withdrawn, closing his office door during the day and leaving work before her to avoid confrontation. Her only saving grace had been a dinner the night before with Ryan. She had cried on his shoulder for hours. Despite his womanizing, he had been warm and caring. He was a lost soul and understood she had screwed up. He had been clear about never taking sides and had told her Mark was pretty destroyed. But somehow knowing he had spoken to Mark made her feel better knowing he was out there and OK.

She looked down at her hand. Yes, it had been stupid to put the ring on. But it was on her right hand so she told herself there was no harm in enjoying it. Knowing Mark and Layla, the two most important people in her life, had picked it out together meant so much to her. It was the most beautiful ring she had ever seen. She knew one day she would need to take it off. It wasn't right to keep it. One day Mark would forgive her and maybe there was a chance they could be friends again. When that day came, she would give him the ring back to give to the next woman that stole his heart.

The wave of nausea hit her hard. Her head spun and she gripped the side of her desk. She stood to run to the bathroom but her legs wouldn't cooperate. Her cubicle blurred and her balance was destroyed. Her last thought before she passed out was of Mark singing at the reception. A song she knew had been for her.

****

Caleb paced the hallway outside the exam room. The smell of alcohol and antiseptic would be permanently engrained in his brain. Sophie had been awake for about thirty minutes and so far, no one had come out to talk to him. The double doors opened and Ryan rushed forward to join him.

"What happened?" His eyes shot in every direction, trying to make sense of the scene before him.

Caleb ran his hand down his face. "I don't know. She had been leaning on her desk and when she stood up, I saw her go down hard. I thought maybe she just tripped but when I came out, she was totally out of it. She was soaked with sweat. The doctor said that she was extremely dehydrated and her pulse was erratic. They are giving her fluids and running some tests but they won't let me in there right now. She is exhausted and hasn't slept for almost a week. I haven't seen her eat anything either."

Ryan put his hand on Caleb's shoulder. "Have you called Mark?"

Caleb shook his head. "He won't take my calls. I don't blame him."

Ryan grabbed his phone from his pocket. On the second ring, Mark's voice came through loud and clear. "Marko, we are up here at Cedars. We don't know anything right now but it's Sophie." The line went dead in his hand.

****

Dr. Garrett Reynolds looked at Sophie and back at the chart in his hands. Clearing his throat, he spoke slowly and quietly. "Ms. Barringer, I am Dr. Reynolds. How is the nausea?"

Sophie looked up from her crackers and attempted a smile. "It's better. I am still pretty dizzy but I think the fluids are helping a lot."

"I have your test results. Your electrolytes are out of balance but the saline should help. Have you been eating?"

Shaking her head no, Sophie spoke. "I have been so

nauseated that I haven't eaten much. I have been trying to drink water but even that makes me sick." As Dr. Reynolds took a seat on the stool next to her, Sophie continued. "I just went through a really tough breakup and I guess it just caught up with me."

"We can give you a little something for the nausea. But I am afraid there isn't much else we can do." Clearing his throat, he put her chart down and looked her in the eye. "Sophie, you are pregnant. Our tests show you are only about four weeks along but I would like to do an ultrasound to make sure everything is going as expected. It's very important that you eat a balanced diet right now. This isn't just about you anymore."

"I'm sorry, what?"

"Your blood work confirms you are four weeks pregnant. Is that the father in the hall?"

Sophie shook her head and tears ran down her cheeks. "How is this possible? I am on the pill. I have been for years." Her hands ran over her belly and she froze. A baby. Oh God, oh God.

"Ms. Barringer, the pill is not 100% effective. And believe it or not, we see a lot of this. I want to do the ultrasound now. Is that ok with you?"

Sophie wiped her face and nodded. A baby. Butterflies erupted in her stomach. A baby. A sob escaped her throat, followed by a laugh. "Yes, I am ready."

****

Mark ran through the door and skidded to a halt in front of Ryan. His face was pale and his hands shook. "What's happening? What happened?"

Caleb rose from the line of chairs across from the exam room and spoke softly. "She passed out at work. We don't know anything else."

Mark spun and faced him. "Oh fucking fantastic. Of course you are here."

Ryan gripped Mark's forearm. "Don't do this here. If he hadn't seen her pass out, who knows what would have happened. We are all here for Sophie and no other reason.

Let's put this to rest just for today."

"They haven't told us anything other than she is dehydrated. She looked terrible man. She scared the hell out of me. She wasn't responsive at all. I'm sorry man. I really am. I did a terrible thing to you and to her. She just needs to be ok." Caleb broke and put his hands on his knees. "She just needs to be ok."

Mark shut his eyes and took a deep breath. "Thank you for finding her. I mean it. Thank you."

The exam room door opened and a nurse stepped out. "Mr. Allen?"

Caleb stood up. "Yes, that's me."

"She is asking for a Mr. Moretti. Could someone call him?"

"I'm Mr. Moretti. Is she ok?" A tear fell down his cheek.

"Yes sir, come with me please." The nurse led Mark into the exam room. "Please have a seat. It is very important not to upset her. Ms. Barringer, are you ok?"

Sophie shook her head and looked at Mark. The flood gates opened and she sobbed. Mark sat on the bed and pulled her into him. "Whatever it is Soph, we can deal with this. Please don't cry."

"I will give you guys a minute. The doctor will be back shortly." The nurse shut the door, shutting Caleb and Ryan on the other side.

Mark looked at Sophie. She was pale and the dark circles under her eyes and her sunken cheeks scared him. "You aren't sleeping."

"Either are you."

Mark kissed her knuckles and sighed. "No. I'm not. It's been a pretty hard week." He wiped another tear from his cheek. "Please Sophie. Please tell me what's happening."

She took a long breath and looked down. Her hands shook. She needed to tell him. If the doctor returned with the ultrasound machine and she had kept quiet, she would be betraying him again. "Mark, I'm so sorry. I don't know how else to tell you except to just say it."

Mark's spine stiffened. "Just say it Sophie. Whatever it is, for the love of God, just say it."

"I'm pregnant."

The room went completely silent. Mark's eyes widened and his jaw dropped. The sound of his panicked breathing and his heart beat was all he heard. Sophie's gaze bore into him trying to gauge any kind of reaction. He had a million. His mind raced. How? When? He should have been more careful. He was pissed. He was thrilled. He needed to forgive her. He couldn't trust her. She was carrying his baby. A baby. No. It couldn't be true. He would die if it was. He would die if it wasn't. He loved her. He was furious with her.

The sound of the door opening again caught his attention. Dr. Reynolds walked through the door with a machine that looked very official. "Sophie, we are going to make sure everything is going according to schedule. Would you like this gentleman to step out?"

Mark stood. "I'm the father. I'm not leaving." The father. Holy shit.

"I'm Dr. Reynolds." He shook Mark's hand. "Our Sophie here has had quite the shock today, as I am sure you have as well. We are going to be doing an ultrasound. Right now the fetus is only about the size of a poppy seed but we should be able to see the gestational sac.

The first twelve weeks of the pregnancy are the most important. If we can get you through that, you have a very good chance of bringing home a healthy baby in about 9 more months. The nurse will make you an appointment with an OBGYN before you leave today so you can ask specific questions at that visit. Shall we get started?"

The ultrasound was invasive and Sophie tried to relax. Mark stared at the screen on the machine. His body was rigid and his breathing shallow. She took his hand and he looked at her. His half smile was more than she expected. Her heart leaped in her chest. This was something that they had created out of love. No matter what was happening to them, they would always be connected and share something so precious. She couldn't hold back her tears..

Dr. Reynolds froze the picture and pointed to the screen. "There. Do you see the gestational sac? That is your baby. And everything is exactly as we expected it would be at four weeks. I will print this for you."

Mark stared. Tears flooded his cheeks. "Our baby." His hand moved to her stomach. "Our baby."

Still in shock, Mark stood and took the black and white grainy image from the doctor. He walked to the doorway and opened it slowly. Ryan and Caleb jumped up from the chairs and froze when they saw his face.

"What's happening. Is she ok?" Caleb rushed to him with Ryan at his heels. "What did the doctor say?"

Without saying a word, Mark handed Ryan the picture and walked to the line of chairs. Ryan stood staring at the picture with wide eyes. Caleb grabbed it and studied it with tears in his eyes. "Holy shit."

Chapter 18

Mark sat at the bar in his new kitchen reading the newspaper. The last few weeks had passed by in a blur. Sophie had been extremely sick but the doctor continued to reassure them this was a good sign. Mark had battled his demons with Caleb and had forgiven him. He understood how easy it was to love Sophie and he couldn't blame his friend for having good taste.

The road to healing with Sophie had been a little harder. Mark knew it would be. His life had been busy with a large contract at work and moving into his new home. Sophie had spent a week on the road with Molly promoting a new book and with her exhaustion, there had been little time to spend together. He had attended both appointments she had with their new doctor and he had called her every night. He still loved her fiercely but his heart was much more guarded. Forgiveness was one thing. Being in love again was something completely different.

Ryan came in from the back porch where he had been on the phone with his boss. "They want me to do an ad campaign for the gym. That's crazy, right?"

Mark looked up from the paper. "Why is it crazy? Do it man. You work hard. Have some fun with it."

Ryan looked around the new kitchen and then back at Mark. "What's with the new ink?

You're going to look like me pretty soon."

Mark chuckled and put the paper away. "Molly calls it my mid life crisis."

The front door slammed and they both jumped. "Hi honey. I'm home."

"Layla?" Mark walked to the kitchen doorway. "What are you doing here? I didn't expect you until tomorrow."

As Layla entered the kitchen, Ryan sat up a little straighter. Something about this woman made him speechless and he did not like being vulnerable. He took a deep breath and smiled as their eyes met.

"How are you Ryan?" Layla winked. She walked to the

refrigerator and took a bottle of water from the top shelf. As she shut the door, the ultrasound picture caught her attention. She removed it from the door and stared dumbstruck. "What the hell is this? Why does it have Sophie's name on it?" When Mark didn't answer, her voice got louder. "What the hell is this? Is this real?"

"Sit." It was a command and Layla followed it. "You are here early. I wasn't expecting to have this talk right now. Or at all."

"Oh my God." Layla's eyes filled with tears. "Mark, is this real?"

Ryan reached over and held her hand. The jolt of electricity was unexpected and Layla stared at him with a blank expression. Mark stood across from her and took the picture back. Placing it back on the refrigerator, he ran his hand over it and smiled. "I thought Sophie would have told you by now."

"I haven't talked to her. I mean, not really. I think we've spoken twice since the wedding and both times have been all about how she messed up, blah blah blah. I haven't even told her I was moving. I thought it would be better in person since she was so depressed. Holy shit. I am going to be an aunt. An Aunt. Are you freaking out? I am freaking out. Wait. Are you together?" Her smile reassured him she was excited.

Mark laughed. Layla had a way of talking forever about

nothing. "No. Not exactly. Hell, I don't know. It's complicated."

Ryan groaned as Layla started speaking. It was obvious he felt the same way. "Well it doesn't need to be. Yank your head out of your ass. If you want to be with her, be with her. Stop tiptoeing around like a scared kid. Claim what is yours. If you don't want her, let it go. But this in between shit is not good for either of you."

Mark put his head on the bar. "You are right. This needs to stop. And no, I am not freaking out. I am someone's dad. That is the most amazing thing in the world."

Layla finished her water and threw the empty bottle at him.

"Come on Ryan. Be my hero and help me get my bags up to my room. Make yourself useful."

Mark grabbed his phone from the counter. 'Can you come by tonight? Any time is fine.'

Her response was simple. 'Yes.'

'I will send you the directions.'

'See you tonight. I miss you Mark.'

Mark smiled. 'I miss you too Soph. You have no idea how much.'

****

Sophie parked her car in front of the massive garage and got out slowly. Was she at the right place? She surveyed the front of the house. Huge. She shook her head and laughed. She had heard very little about the house and she was shocked to see the massive structure in front of her. Several moving boxes were thrown onto the front porch. "This must be it," she mumbled to herself as she rang the door bell.

Mark answered the door in a bathing suit, hair wet from a swim. "Hey beautiful. Come in. I'm sorry. I was hoping I had time to take a shower before you got here." He kissed her on the cheek and led her into the foyer. "Want a tour?"

Sophie gasped at the marble floors and large staircase. "Yes." Her voice was breathless. "This is amazing Mark."

He held her hand and led her through the first floor. He pointed out the pool and view with a smile on his face and continued into the kitchen and even showed her the garage. Moving to the second floor, he pointed out several bedrooms and bathrooms and an office. He quickly pointed into the master bedroom as his nerves got the better of him. "And this, well, I thought this could be the nursery. I am right next door and it gets morning sun and has a beautiful view for the middle of the night feedings."

Sophie smiled and leaned into him. "It is perfect. Just perfect. I couldn't have picked anything any better."

Mark wrapped his arms around her and she let out the breath she had been holding. He pulled her tightly against his chest and kissed her neck. "I'm glad you like it. I picked it for you." Her body stiffened and he smiled. "Come on. There is one more room. There is a small third floor that has a bedroom and a bathroom and a nice balcony."

Sophie stopped outside the closed door of the third floor room. Mark paused and knocked and she gave him a questioning look. "I got us a live in babysitter so we can have a life. If you want one I mean."

The door opened and Sophie squealed. "Layla. What are you doing here?"

Layla pulled her into a big hug and then dropped to her knees and spoke to her belly. "Hi baby. Your daddy thought you might need to have your aunt around to teach you all the things your mommy and daddy don't think you should know. I will be here for as long as you need me"

Sophie looked at Mark. Her tears flowed down her cheeks and she laughed. "She lives here?" Mark nodded and smiled. She jumped into his arms. "Thank you Mark."

As she held him, the walls he had put up all crashed to the ground. His future was so clear. She was everything he wanted. "Sit. Talk. I am going to take a shower and then we can have some dinner and talk."

****

Sophie snuck into the master bedroom and shut the door. She kicked her shoes under the bed and pulled her sundress over her head. The sound of the shower came from the half closed bathroom door. She pushed her way in and smiled. The glass enclosed shower gave her a view of the most beautiful man she had ever seen. He had added some tattoos to his chest and arms and she couldn't wait to trace them all with her tongue. The man was pure heaven. Just the thought of him turned her on. His muscles rippled as he shampooed his hair and turned his face into the stream of water.

Sophie opened the shower door and walked in. She reached out to touch his shoulder and he jumped. "Stay just like that." She grabbed the soap and washed his back and shoulders. When she got to his arms, she kissed the new artwork. "This is nice."

Mark cleared his throat. "Sophie, what are you doing?" He turned around to face her.

Her hands went right to the stars on his chest and traced them lightly. "I miss you. I miss kissing you and holding you. I miss your touch. I don't want to be without you anymore."

Mark swept her into his arms and kissed her. His kiss was slow and loving. Sophie squirmed in his arms wanting to be closer to him. She would never be able to be close enough. She ran her hands down his back and dug her nails into his ass. He moaned into her mouth.

Breaking the kiss, she dropped to her knees and before he could stop her, she took his length into her mouth. Her hands and mouth worked in perfect harmony rubbing up and down his shaft. His breathing became strained. "Jesus Sophie." His hands slapped onto the sides of the shower stall. She smiled as she looked up at him and teased him as she took him into her mouth again. He closed his eyes and groaned. Her mouth was so warm. When he realized he couldn't wait any longer, he tugged her to her feet.

"I need to be inside you." He turned the water off and picked her up. She wrapped her arms and legs around him and sucked the water from his neck. He put her down gently in front of the bathroom mirror and bent her over. "This is room one. I plan to have you in every room of this house."

He eased into her from behind and sighed. Her eyes met his in the mirror as he started to thrust into her. Her face was flushed. She smiled a sexy smile at him as he picked up speed. Reaching around her, he circled her clit with his fingers. She bit her bottom lip but kept eye contact with him. Her movement became more frantic and he knew she was close. He pinched her nipple with his other hand and bit her shoulder. She came apart around him, clenching him with her slick walls. Her legs buckled but he held her up. "Not yet. You aren't done yet." Her hooded eyes met his again. More moisture pooled around him and he grabbed her hair and pulled back lightly. She moaned. "You like that baby?"

She nodded and found her voice. "God yes. Harder Mark. I need more."

"What do you want baby?" His strokes slowed as he waited for an answer. "Tell me."

"I want to turn around." She smiled as she remembered their time together in the ocean. "I want to turn around and kiss you while you make love to me. I want you to make me come again."

Mark pulled out of her, threw her onto the counter and eased into her again. He held her close, his lips meeting hers with urgency. He tilted her head back and his tongue thrust deeper in her throat. She moaned. She took his hand and put it on her over sensitive bundle of nerves. She circled his fingers with hers and threw her head back. "God yes. That feels so good."

Her release was almost immediate and she screamed his name as he thrust into her two more times. His orgasm was so powerful; he grabbed the counter to keep from losing his balance. His body shuttered with each final thrust.

He lifted her from the counter and carried her to the bedroom. Their bodies were slick with sweat. He winked as he climbed on top of her on the bed. "I know we should probably clean up. But, I'm not done with you yet."

She pulled him down and kissed him hard. She nibbled on his bottom lip and ran her tongue down his neck. "I know you might not be ready to hear this, but I love you."

He sighed. "I am always ready to hear that. I love you so much Sophie."

"Can I stay with you tonight?"

His smile lit up his face. "Sophie, as far as I'm concerned, you never have to leave."

Epilogue

3 months later

Mark stood on his front porch. The sun was beginning to set earlier and the evenings were becoming cooler. His briefcase fell from his hands and he pressed his head against the door. The day had been filled with one work crisis after another and he couldn't wait to throw on his swimsuit, lap out his frustration, then spend the evening holding Sophie.

Her morning sickness had completely resolved and as she hit the second trimester, her energy had come racing back. She hadn't given up her apartment but her things had slowly made their way into Mark's home. Aside from Mark's trip back east for business, Sophie had spent every night making love to him and reminding him why they belonged together. The relationship had become more than she ever imagined.

Mark stepped into the dark foyer and took a deep breath. The sounds of footsteps on the stairs made him look up. "Why are you here and more importantly, why were you upstairs?"

Caleb tensed as he noticed Mark standing in the doorway. He looked around and stuttered. "I, uh, just came by to say hello to you guys."

"Ok. Doesn't explain why you were upstairs Allen." Mark set his briefcase on the bench by the door and loosened his tie. "Start explaining before I take the frustrations of my day out on you."

A second pair of feet appeared in Mark's vision and Ryan stumbled into Caleb's back. "What's up Marco?" Ryan, always calm and collected, looked around in a panic.

"Start explaining you two. And I mean now." Mark rubbed his hand over his face and tried to take a few steps upstairs. Ryan blocked his way. "Dude. I am seriously exhausted. I just want to put on my swim trunks and relax."

Caleb jogged past them both, into the living room and out the back door. There were hushed voices and a loud crash. Mark turned toward the sliding glass door as Ryan stepped into his face. "Give it just a minute man. Please." Ryan loosened his grip.

Mark groaned. "It's been a shit day. What's going on?"

Sophie stepped through the back door, her smile radiant. Her hair was pulled off her face in a low ponytail and her tanned legs ended in a pair of strappy sandals. She fixed the waist of her sundress as she stepped toward Mark. "Hi baby. I missed you." Her kiss was soft and she melted into his embrace.

Smiling against her neck, he whispered. "You smell good. What's going on?"

She laughed. "My pathetic attempt at a surprise. You are early." She took his hand and led him out the back door.

Candles floated in the pool and the large dining table was set. Rich cooked steaks and vegetables on the grill and the bar was set up with every drink imaginable. Molly, Caleb, Layla, Mr. and Mrs. Dickerman, his mother and Chad sat at the table. Mark looked around at his guests and then back at Sophie. "What is this?"

Sophie led him to the seat at the head of the table and sat down in his lap. "You have been working so hard and I just wanted you to know how much we all love you. I wanted to have everyone over for dinner and drinks. Kind of a housewarming. Are you mad?"

Mark smiled and kissed her. "No baby. I'm not mad. I'm

thrilled." He stood and greeted all his guests and grabbed a beer from the bar. Ryan handed him a shot of tequila and he threw it back. His exhaustion disappeared with each sip.

Looking back at Sophie, he relaxed. She was beautiful. If he had been able to ask for everything he had ever wanted, it would have been wrapped in a package just like Sophie. His life was complete.

He ran his hand over the engagement ring in his pocket. He had taken the original ring and had it reset. There had been too many bad memories surrounding the first one. His plan was to ask her to marry him tonight during a moonlit swim. They loved the pool and he couldn't think of anything more romantic than under the stars in their own private paradise.

Sophie stood up and grabbed a folded paper off the bar. "This is for you."

He opened it. "Your lease?"

She laughed. "My broken lease. I'm moving in this weekend." She squealed as Mark picked her up and swung her around. "I take it you are happy?"

Ryan gagged. "Seriously bro. I don't know how the hell this happened to you. I honestly miss my wing man. But I couldn't be happier for you."

Sophie hit him in the arm. "Like you aren't sniffing around a certain brunette that shall remain nameless? Please. You haven't been out in two weeks."

Mark looked from Sophie to Ryan. "Who?"

Ryan chugged his beer and looked at Layla. "Another story for another night."

"Steaks are done. Come to the table kids." Rich laughed as he put a tray of steaks in the center of the table.

Mark looked at all the faces that were most important to him in the world. Mr. and Mrs. Dickerman were like parents to him. They had helped raise him and helped make him the man he had become. His mother was there with a smile on her face despite the fact that his father was once again on the road. Ryan had taken a seat by Layla and was currently getting the cold shoulder. He wondered about those two and he looked forward to whatever the future would bring them. Molly and Rich had settled into married life beautifully. They were completely in love and had found out several days before that they were expecting a baby. Mark and Molly would have children that would grow up together, just like they had. His heart swelled and his eyes watered.

He realized Sophie was standing up and the rest of the table was quiet, looking at him. "I'm sorry. What?"

Sophie smiled. "I was wondering if you could have a seat. I have something to say."

Her hands shook as she straightened her dress.

Mark walked to the table and sat down. He looked up at Sophie. She was breathless and blushing fiercely.

She looked down at him and began. "A year ago, I had given up on everything good in my life. Then a really stubborn woman pulled me up from the gutter and made me open my eyes to all kinds of wonderful things. Asking me to be her maid of honor has proven to be the most important thing in the world." She cleared her throat. "It was an accident that I was at the grocery store that day. I was running late and wasn't paying any attention, when I rammed my cart into the ankles of the most amazing man I had ever seen. Since that day, not one second has passed that I haven't thought of him or missed him or loved him. He became the most amazing thing that has ever happened to me and the absolute most important person in my life. I love you every single minute of every single day. I would be nothing without you."

She knelt down next to him and his eyes widened. "I have made some mistakes. I have been dumb and blind. But through everything, you have been my rock. I don't know how I got so lucky but if you will let me, I am going to spend the rest of my life thanking God that you took a chance on me."

She slipped a gold ring from her thumb and held it up to him. "In front of everyone that is most special to us in the world, I am asking you the most important question I will ever ask anyone."

Mark dropped to his knees and put his finger across her lips. "No Sophie." As the table gasped, he continued. "I am the lucky one. The day you hit me with that cart was the day that I completely lost my heart to you. I never thought I would find love. I never even knew I wanted to. But that day, with your messy hair and your workout clothes and your clumsy apology, I knew my life would never be the same."

He pulled the diamond ring from his pocket and held it to her. A shower of light spilled onto the pavement as the candles reflected off the diamond. "I love you Sophie Barringer. And I love this wonderful life we are going to bring into the world. I love waking up next to you and holding you as you fall asleep. I love fighting over the crossword or who gets the last bite of ice cream. But most of all, I love the man I am because you took a chance on loving me." He looked around the table at all the people who had made him the person he had become. "Life has truly blessed me. And without you, I would be lost. Sophie, will you do me the amazing honor of becoming my wife?"

She pulled him in for a kiss. "Yes," she whispered. And as the world disappeared around them, he knew that his life would never be the same.

The End.

Acknowledgments

This book was an emotional journey for me. I wrote it in bed while I was recovering from my second back surgery in two months. What a blessing that time turned out to be. (Thank you Dr. G for giving me my life back after my injury) In such a short period of time, I learned about who I am, what I want and who would stand by my side. It was an amazing journey and I wouldn't have traded it for anything in the world.

I want to thank my husband who single parented through my recovery and allowed me to steal his laptop every night. Thank you for giving me the time to heal. Thank you for allowing me the quiet moments to write. And most of all, thank you for our gorgeous daughter. (Who I hope will never ever ever read this) Thank you for the past nine years and I look forward to growing old(er) with you.

To my mom, my favorite writer in the world. You gave me a life that people only dream about. You opened your heart and adopted a little baby girl and our bond far exceeds any bond of blood. My life has been amazing because I was chosen to be yours. Your unconditional love made me the person I am today. Thank you for sharing your love of art and books and encouraging me to dream big. I love you.

Dad & Chris. I hope you don't ever read this book. But thank you for being OK with me writing under my maiden name, the one you have to live with everyday while I can hide behind my married one. After all, Carnal is totally appropriate. It was write Adult fiction or be a doctor. I think I chose wisely. I had amazing men to look up to growing up. Thank you for that. Thank you for the millions of times you have both saved me and all the lessons I learned from you. (Even if some of them came with some big brother torture)

I also would like to thank Ashley, my beta reader, fashion advisor and superwoman extraordinaire. Thank you for stalking me every night for new chapters and for keeping all the characters straight for me. Thank you for all the dinners and visits during my recovery and for standing by my side through everything from the first day we met. This was an adventure and I would not have wanted to take it with anyone else but you.

Alex Michael Turner!!! THANK YOU THANK YOU. For being my cover model and my muse and a huge inspiration to me while I was going through all the hell with my back. You ARE my Mark Moretti. There is no one else I would have wanted on this cover. Thank you for allowing me to be a part of the cover shoot and for the most amazing time in Portland. It is an honor to call you a friend. You are the most humble, trusting and loving person. I have told you before that I think you are an old soul. The perfect gentleman. THANK YOU. You are pure inspiration. I can't wait to see where life takes you. Find Alex on Facebook at www.facebook.com/alexmichaelturner

Eric Wainwright. I love our daily chats and all the pictures I get to see before they are posted. You make me laugh everyday. Thank you for the red couch picture that honestly started all of this. You are so talented (and tall) and I cannot wait to watch your career sky rocket! You rock! Thank you for the cover photo. (And the covers yet to come) My life is better because you are in it. You amaze me. Find Eric on Facebook at www.facebook.com/wainwrightimages

A huge thank you and cyber hug to Nickie Seidler, author of A Lucky Second Chance. This was so much fun to share with you. Even though it was sometimes the blind leading the blind, I loved having someone reading my book from an author's perspective. And I can't help but giggle at how jealous I got that you loved Mark so much. Thank you for trusting me with your manuscript (and Nathan!) and for keeping mine safe.

And to all the readers, Facebook followers, new authors and book lovers. Everyday I wake up and meet someone amazing that I hadn't known the day before. Your support is felt and I appreciate you more than you will ever know. Thank you for loving Mark Moretti and I look forward to sharing the other Moretti/Dickerman brothers with you. Authors write to create the world of their dreams. Thank you for supporting us and for wanting to be a part of the world we create. YOU ARE LOVED!

About the Author

MJ Carnal lives in Lexington, South Carolina with her husband, gorgeous daughter and two loving and super furry dogs. She spends her days in the world of neurosurgery but her nights in a world she creates on paper. When she isn't writing, you can find her watching episodes of The Walking Dead with her hubby, having tea parties with Princess Caroline, Singing karaoke for anyone that will listen and reading just about anything she can get her hands on. "Taming the Bachelor" is her first published book but her first series was written at the age of eight and illustrated with crayon. Look for the next book, "Taming the Playboy" early fall 2013.

She loves to hear from fans, fellow writers and book lovers. Find her online at www.facebook.com/mjcarnalauthor or on Twitter @mjcarnalauthor.

Stay tuned for more in the Dickerman Moretti series

"Taming the Playboy" – The story of Ryan West, late summer 2013

"Taming the Boy Next Door" – The story of Caleb Allen, Fall 2013

"Taming Casanova" – The story of Kevin Merck, Winter 2013

Taming the Playboy – Late Summer 2013

Taming the Playboy – Chapter 1

Ryan pulled his shirt over his head and wrapped his towel around his neck. His ten mile run did little to clear his head. His muscles ached but nothing compared to the ache in his chest where his heart beat its betrayal. Pulling a bottle of water from the refrigerator, he opened the cap and chugged the entire thing. Her memory haunted him.

He ran his hand through his sweaty, dark hair and threw his Red Sox cap onto his desk. He knew this was nonsense. His days of partying with multiple women were his trademark. There was never just one that stuck with him. He growled as he sat down at his desk. "This is ridiculous," he mumbled to himself.

It was simple. He lived by three rules. The first and most important rule, never get attached. The second rule, work hard but play harder. And the third, one night stands meant one night. He didn't do relationships. That was plain and simple. The only commitments he made were to his family and to his group of friends. If you didn't fit into one of those groups, Ryan West was not a permanent fixture in your life.

"I know that look." Kevin Merck threw his towel at Ryan. "And I have never seen that look on your face before. Who is she?"

Ryan looked up at his coworker and laughed. "You have lost your mind, dude. There isn't a woman in this world that could make me have whatever look you think I have."

"It happens to the best of us, man." Kevin laughed as he sorted the mail into stacks.

"It doesn't happen to me. That is a well known fact. You forget who you are talking to."

"Give me a break, West. I haven't seen you hit a club or a chick in months." Ryan shrugged and picked up his mail. "Here. Enjoy." Kevin threw a magazine on his desk and left the office.

Ryan held the August edition of Los Angeles Confidential

Magazine and smiled. Staring back from the front cover was a picture of him, taken during a photo shoot a few months prior. He chuckled as he read the article.

Ryan West had moved to Los Angeles at the age of eleven. After his diagnosis of Leukemia, his parents felt that they should leave the suburbs of Boston for a more holistic approach to a cure. He had spent the first six months of his time in Los Angeles visiting healers, having acupuncture and massage and becoming more ill. When the doctors gave his family the grim news that the Leukemia was not responding, he underwent chemotherapy and a bone marrow transplant. His life had been turned upside down. A whole year had been lost to aggressive treatments and after spending his sixth grade year in a hospital bed, he vowed to never take life for granted.

Completely bald and with a battered body, Ryan took the halls of Beverly Vista Middle school by storm. His first day of school, he met a very outspoken Mark Moretti, a very wild Caleb Allen and very reserved Rich Dickerman and became a permanent fixture of what the teachers called the Dickerman Brothers. He excelled at sports and academics and even at a young age, his focus on healthy living never wavered. His zest for life was matched only by his love of the opposite sex. He made a pact with his friends that they would live the high life together, promising to maintain bachelor status for life. It seemed like such a simple idea to a young mind.

Ryan attended UCLA on a baseball scholarship and set his sites on the major leagues and the Boston Red Sox. His sophomore year began with a health scare that required five rounds of chemotherapy and the end of his college career. Being unable to play baseball, his scholarship was dissolved and Ryan spent the remainder of what would have been his college days, living with Caleb and Mark and studying physical therapy at the local community college. He had made a career out of physical fitness and had become one of the most popular trainers in LA.

Los Angeles Confidential had asked to interview him when they learned of some of his famous clients and the difference Ryan was making through his non profit foundation, Save LA Youth. The reporter had taken one look at him and fallen hard. His pictures scattered the pages of the article and adorned the front page.

The cell phone rang and startled him. "Ryan West."

Mark's voice yelled through the phone. "How is my favorite celebrity today? Just picked up my copy of the magazine and walked right off the curb when I saw your ugly mug staring back at me. Why didn't you tell us you got the cover?"

Ryan laughed. "I hope you twisted your ankle."

"Is that any way to talk to the man who has four tables reserved at Foxtail for tonight at 8:00? Dinner and drinks on me and Sophie. We will see you there." Mark hung up without waiting for a response.

"You have plans tonight Kev?" Ryan yelled out into the gym. "Dinner and Drinks at 8. I need a new wingman."

Tonight, he would get her out of his system. Tonight he would cuddle up to a warm body and remind himself that he was a playboy. It was now or never. Ryan scrubbed his hand down his face. He hoped she wouldn't be there.

****

Ryan stepped into Foxtail right on time. His jeans hung low on his hips, showing off his narrow waist. His red shirt hugged his shoulders and his muscles rippled underneath. His dark hair stuck up on top, like he had just gotten out of bed and his brown eyes sparkled when he smiled. He turned heads everywhere he went. He spent more nights than he could count bedding his female admirers and had a black book full of midnight calls he could count on.

Spotting his friends in the corner, Ryan waved. He ordered a beer and took a seat next to Mark. Surveying the table, he took in all the smiling faces. When his gaze landed on Layla, he had to swallow around the lump in his throat. This was going to be a long night.

"Congrats brother. We had no idea we were in the company of a VIP."

"Bite me Moretti." Ryan took a long pull of his beer. "I have been telling you assholes for years that I am a legend."

"And he's humble." Layla smiled and held up her beer as his friends laughed. "I guess I need a personal trainer since I now live in the land of the beautiful."

"Lay, you don't need any help." Mark put his arm around his soon to be sister in law.

Ryan felt an overwhelming urge to growl. His lips formed a straight line and his eyes narrowed. The green eyed monster had reared its ugly head and had taken a seat in

Ryan's lap. Clearing his throat, Ryan looked at Layla. "I will help you anytime. I'm in the gym until six everyday and then can be wherever you need me, whenever you need me."

"That almost sounded like a come on. And seriously, Ryan, you cannot get near my sister. I won't let that happen." Sophie sipped her water and rubbed her slightly rounded, pregnant belly.

Layla made eye contact with Ryan and blushed. Their secret was safe for now. But he knew they could never make that mistake again. He would never settle down. He lived life to the fullest and that did not include being tied down to one person. And Layla was different. Her love of adventure and family made her the perfect woman, for someone else. She loved children and had dedicated her life to being an interpreter for hearing disabled youth. He would not have children. He had watched his parents go through his illness with heavy hearts and a broken bank account. He would not pass his genes down to another person.

The conversation turned to the article and his dedication to the youth of LA. His program had provided free healthcare to the less fortunate. He worked side by side with the same doctors that had saved his life nearly fifteen years before. Countless people worked tirelessly to make sure the underprivileged had preventative health screenings and if cancer was detected, Ryan made sure he was available as a role model during treatment. Layla had listened and held her breath as she heard the story of his Leukemia. Her face had paled as she heard about the diagnosis and the difficult time his family had during treatment. She had winked at him when he made eye contact and watched him when he wasn't looking.

After more shots than Ryan could count and a belly full of terrible food, he stood and made his way to the back of the club. His mind had stayed focused on Layla all evening. He had watched her mouth as she spoke and her tongue as she licked her lips. Her dark eyes had met him a few times and held. His temperature had risen and his pants had become tight. When he couldn't breathe, he excused himself to go splash some cold water on his face. It hadn't helped. His brain was in overdrive. It had been nearly eight weeks since the encounter in Layla's room and there had been no one since. His reputation for a new woman every night had gone out the window with one touch of her skin. It was time to move on. He took a deep breath and headed to the door.

As he walked down the dark hallway, gentle hands grabbed his shirt and pressed him against the wall. With total abandon, Layla's lips crashed against his and her tongue begged for entry. He moaned into her mouth and parted his lips. She wrapped her arms tightly around his neck and her tongue thrust into his mouth. She pulled his bottom lip with her teeth and when he tried to move, he found himself plastered against the wall once more.

"Layla," He breathed. His breath was shallow and his heart pounded against his rib cage. "What are you doing?"

"I want you. Right now. No more games." She pulled him from the wall and into the door marked 'employees only'. She turned the lock on the door and pulled her shirt over her head. He lifted her and she wrapped her legs around his waist. She rubbed her body over his jeans and moaned. Unbuttoning his jeans, she whispered. "Let's do this."

"Shit yeah," Ryan moaned.

He lifted her skirt to her waist. He pushed aside her black silk thong and his fingers drove into her with abandon. She gasped and gripped his shoulders. Her mouth crashed to his lips and their tongues tangled in an urgent dance. His fingers pulsed inside her, bending slightly and pushing on the place deep inside her that set her on fire. Her orgasm ripped from her without warning, soaking his fingers and she slumped against him.

"God baby. I don't think I could ever get enough of that." Ryan panted against her neck.

"Don't talk." Layla handed him a foil packet and he ripped it open. She shoved his jeans down to his thighs and positioned her core over his impossibly hard length. She moaned as she took all of him. Her slick core tingled as he filled her. She bit her bottom lip as he began pounding into her.

As her second orgasm rocked her, she bit his shoulder and he growled. Her body pulsed around him, squeezing him and encouraging him to let go. His breath became ragged as he pumped into her two more times before erupting with his own pleasure. Heat poured between them and his hungry mouth found hers again. He moaned as her tongue slipped into his mouth.

With shaking hands, he set her back on the floor and fixed her skirt. "We need to stop doing this, Ryan. I know we do. But I can't help myself." Layla smoothed the front of his shirt and sighed. "What do you want to do?"

"I want to take you home. And I have never taken anyone home before."

On her tip toes, she kissed him softly and purred. "I would like that."

With his heart in his throat, Ryan watched as she walked away.

Made in the USA
Charleston, SC
24 February 2014